"I'd hate to be a third wheel."

"Technically, you'd be the fourth wheel," Rick corrected Emma, adding a mischievous grin. "And if you want to come, we'd love to have you. The girls, I mean," he amended quickly.

"What about you?"

"What about me?"

"Are you honestly that clueless, or are you just messing with me?"

He laughed out loud. "Okay, you got me. It's nice to have another grown-up to talk to, and you're great company."

"Really? But I'm so quiet."

"And funny and sweet. I have to say, I've never met anyone quite like you, Emma. You're one of a kind."

"Does that work on the other women you've known?"

Suddenly, the humor left his expression. "Only one."

"Sarah?" When he nodded, she steadied her voice. "I'm honored. May I ask you something?"

"Sure."

"Do you think you'll ever be able to think of her and smile?"

He took a moment to consider that and nodded. "Someday. People tell me the pain eases, but I didn't believe that. Until recently, anyway."

Mia Ross loves great stories. She enjoys reading about fascinating people, long-ago times and exotic places. But only for a little while, because her reality is pretty sweet. Married to her college sweetheart, she's the proud mom of two amazing kids, whose schedules keep her hopping. Busy as she is, she can't imagine trading her life for anyone else's—and she has a pretty good imagination. You can visit her online at miaross.com.

Books by Mia Ross

Love Inspired

Liberty Creek

Mending the Widow's Heart
The Bachelor's Baby
His Two Little Blessings

Oaks Crossing

Her Small-Town Cowboy
Rescued by the Farmer
Hometown Holiday Reunion
Falling for the Single Mom

Barrett's Mill

Blue Ridge Reunion
Sugar Plum Season
Finding His Way Home
Loving the Country Boy

Visit the Author Profile page at Harlequin.com for more titles.

His Two Little Blessings

Mia Ross

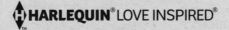

Recycling programs
for this product may
not exist in your area.

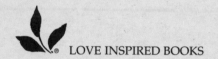

LOVE INSPIRED BOOKS

ISBN-13: 978-1-335-42820-2

His Two Little Blessings

www.Harlequin.com

Printed in U.S.A.

For with God nothing shall be impossible.
—*Luke* 1:37

This one's for you, Dad.

I miss you every day.

Acknowledgments

To Melissa Endlich and the dedicated staff at Love Inspired. These very talented folks help me make my books everything they can be.

More thanks to the gang at Seekerville (www.seekerville.blogspot.com), a great place to hang out with readers—and writers.

I've been blessed with a wonderful network of supportive, encouraging family and friends. You inspire me every day!

Chapter One

"Miss Calhoun! Miss Calhoun!"

At the sound of a child's voice calling out her name, Emma looked into the crowd milling around the annual Liberty Creek Arts and Crafts Show. It was a gorgeous New Hampshire day in early May, and there were dozens of kids in the tree-shaded square who might have shouted to her. Being the elementary school's only art teacher, she knew most of the young ones in town, so it could have been any one of them.

Then she caught sight of a little girl running toward her stand near the white gazebo, hand waving enthusiastically in the air, a riot of blond curls bouncing behind her. When she stopped in front of Emma's jewelry stand, her cheeks were pink from the exercise, her china-blue eyes shining in excitement as she exhaled a breathless "Hello."

"Hello to you, too, Caitlin," Emma replied, stepping out to give the bright kindergartener a hug. "I'm so glad you found me."

"There's a lot of people here," she agreed, glancing around before looking back at Emma. "But my daddy's tall, so he saw you from way over there."

She pointed to the edge of the park, and Emma followed the motion to see Rick Marshall, the bank's new assistant manager, moving toward them, carrying a smaller version of Caitlin in his arms. They'd met a few times at school functions, but she'd never spent more than a few minutes chatting with him. Wearing khaki shorts and a dark blue polo shirt, he had the look of someone who spent his days in suits and ties and was happy to be dressed down for the weekend.

The sun picked up some highlights in his brown hair, not to mention the color of his eyes that echoed his daughters'. His wife was a very fortunate woman, Emma mused as he joined them. "Good afternoon, Mr. Marshall. How are you today?"

"Just fine," he replied with an easy smile.

"And I know I've told you at least twice to call me Rick."

Emma made it a policy to address her students' parents—especially the good-looking fathers—in a formal way that couldn't possibly be misinterpreted as flirting. Being twenty-six and single was hard enough without creating the kind of wrong impression that could earn her a reprimand from the district superintendent or a complaint from a jealous wife.

So she ignored the chiding and focused on the adorable cherub he held. "You must be Aubrey. Caitlin has told me a lot about you during art class, but it's nice to finally meet you in person."

The child gave her a bashful half smile before burying her head in her father's chest.

"She's a little shy," Caitlin explained, patting her sister's back in a comforting way that said she did it often. "Being four is scary."

"It certainly is," Emma confirmed, directing her comments to the older girl to avoid frightening the younger one. "Even grown-ups get scared about new things sometimes. That's why it's good to have a family watching out for you."

They chatted about school and the new friends Caitlin had made since starting there during the winter term. After a couple of minutes Aubrey swiveled her face toward the conversation, clearly interested in what they were saying. Emma was careful not to look directly at the reserved child, but from Rick's pleased expression, she guessed that Aubrey was slowly warming up to her. Being on the timid side herself, Emma hated it when people tried to force her to participate in a discussion when she wasn't ready. She could definitely relate to Aubrey's cautious approach to the world around her.

"So," Rick said when their small talk died down, "when I stopped by Liberty Creek Forge to pick up my new garden gate the other day, your brother Brian was telling me that you make jewelry and you'd be selling some of it here today. Do you mind if we take a look?"

"Not a bit," she replied, stepping back to give them a clear path to her booth. "Also, I keep forgetting to thank you for helping Brian out with the financing for his business. He never would've gotten started if you hadn't stepped in to smooth things over for him with the loan committee."

"Everyone deserves a chance to succeed," Rick said, shifting Aubrey to his other side so she could look down at the array of necklaces that Caitlin was admiring. "Brian's a good guy, and Lindsay's an expert at keeping her husband and the business on track, so I felt they were a good risk. From what I see here, there's quite a bit of artistic talent in the Calhoun family."

It was flattering to hear that, but Emma felt her cheeks heating with embarrassment. She'd never been comfortable being complimented for something that she considered to be a gift from God, a talent meant to be shared with others who could appreciate it. Strangers often mistook her reticence for standoffishness, so she forced herself to smile up at the tall banker. "That's nice of you to say. Thank you."

"Just stating a fact, but you're welcome. We're looking for a Mother's Day gift for my mom. What do you think she'd like, girls?"

The two of them debated over several items before finally settling on a pretty beaded bracelet with a silver oval that read "Grandma." While Emma boxed and wrapped it for them, she asked, "Do you see anything your mommy might like?"

In a heartbeat, the three Marshalls fell silent. Rick's jaw tightened in obvious distress, and he pulled Aubrey a bit closer, resting a hand on Caitlin's shoulder in a protective gesture that told Emma she'd inadvertently stumbled onto very sensitive ground. Feeling awful, she wished there was a way to un-ask her question.

Lifting large, sad eyes to hers, in a voice barely above a whisper, Caitlin said, "Mommy's in heaven."

Unbidden, Emma's gaze fell on Rick's left hand, which still bore a gold wedding band. With great determination, she raised her eyes to meet his and frowned. "I'm so sorry. I had no idea."

"We try to keep it to ourselves, for the girls' sake," he explained tersely. "Fewer questions to answer that way."

Nodding, she tried desperately to come up with something else to say. Nothing comforting came to mind, so she simply said, "I understand."

"Thank you."

The casual ease that he'd displayed earlier had vanished, and in its place stood a man who was clearly still grieving, even while he raised his two beautiful daughters. Emma's family was as close-knit as they came, and she couldn't imagine how her life would be without her own mother. When trouble had come to her two years ago, the first person she'd confided in was Mom. They'd had a good cry, then got to work figuring out how to handle her sobering diagnosis.

Leukemia, the doctor had somberly informed her. Stage three.

Her family's unwavering support, and a lot of prayer, had gotten Emma through the worst time of her life. The tests and seemingly endless rounds of chemo had gone on for months, and there had been times when she honestly thought she couldn't possibly endure any more. She'd pushed away the despair, armed with a collection of cute hats and handmade jewelry that had spawned a new hobby that helped to keep her sane throughout her treatment.

In the end, she'd gotten through it using equal measures of grit and faith. Now, hopefully, she was on the other side of it and moving forward. The date of her follow-up test was circled on her calendar in bright pink. It was a cheerful, upbeat color, and she hoped her results would warrant it.

An optimist by nature, she'd learned the hard way that a positive attitude wasn't always enough to make things work out in her favor. And while she recognized that it was important to be prepared for the worst, she didn't know what that might be.

She'd never summoned the courage to ask.

* * *

Rick had no clue what to say next.

To cover his sudden silence, he set Aubrey down in the lush spring grass and pulled out his wallet. To Caitlin, he said, "Why don't you two go across the aisle to Mrs. Calhoun's stand and get us all some cookies and lemonade?"

"Okay, Daddy," Caitlin agreed, nodding as if she understood that the conversation he was about to have wasn't one for young ears. Taking Aubrey's hand, she smiled and gave a light tug. "Come on. Let's go get a snack."

When he was satisfied that the girls were out of earshot, he squared his shoulders and faced the art teacher, who'd so innocently punched him in the gut. Her vivid blue eyes were filled with sympathy, made even more intense by the sunlight streaming down through the branches overhead. Her honey-brown hair shifted in the warm breeze, and she toyed with a short piece in a gesture that made it clear she was as uncomfortable as he was.

"About the ring…" The opening sounded awkward, and he felt more like a teenager approaching his crush to ask for a date than a twenty-eight-year-old man about to impose some logic on what must seem odd.

"There's no need to explain yourself to me,

Mr. Marshall," she assured him in a formal tone very unlike the one she'd been using with him up until now. "What you wear or don't wear is your own business. I'm just sorry that I misunderstood your situation. Being a single father is hard enough, but your circumstances are heartbreaking. I feel awful for upsetting you and the girls this way."

Amazing, he thought with true admiration. Any other woman would have been curious about why he still wore his wedding ring when he was no longer married. Enough had done it recently that he'd come to expect the question. Despite the strain he was feeling, Emma's respect for his wishes brushed some of his discomfort away.

"Sarah and I got married right after we finished college and had Caitlin a year later," he explained quietly, hoping to avoid sharing his painful personal history with the people browsing at the next table. "When Aubrey was born four years ago, Sarah didn't bounce back the way she did after Caitlin. For a few months she chalked the fatigue up to being a full-time mother of two."

He heard the catch in his voice and paused to steady it. To his surprise, Emma laid a reassuring hand on his arm. "You don't need to keep going if you'd rather not. I can fill in the blanks on my own."

"Really?"

She nodded. "When Caitlin first started at school, my hair was still coming back in and I wore a lot of hats. She mentioned that her mother had done the same thing, so I assumed she'd been through something similar. I just didn't realize that she passed away, and I'm truly sorry for all you and the girls have lost. They're both wonderful, and Sarah must have been a remarkable woman to give them so much before she died."

"She was," he confirmed, relieved to feel his emotional balance returning. Emma's soft voice, coupled with the compassionate words that she'd offered to him, eased the tension he'd been fighting, and he dredged up a smile for the kind woman. "Thank you for understanding."

"Of course."

The girls returned with their snack—most of it, anyway—and Rick turned his attention to a less morbid topic. "I'm seeing partial cookies and half-filled cups. Did you run into the Cookie Monster between here and there?"

"No, Daddy," Aubrey replied, laughing at

his reference to one of her favorite characters. "We were hungry."

"But we saved one for you," Caitlin added, pulling it from the pocket of her sundress to hand it to him. And then, reaching back in, she pulled another to offer her teacher. "And this is for you. Your grandma said it's your favorite."

"It's a raccoon," Aubrey chirped helpfully.

"Macaroon," Rick corrected her with a chuckle. "And it looks delicious. Did you thank Mrs. Calhoun when you paid her?"

Caitlin's eyes widened guiltily, and she took the money he'd given her from her other pocket. Giving it back to him, she confessed, "We were talking about what I'm doing at school, and I forgot. I'll go back and give it to her."

"Don't worry about it," Emma told her with a laugh. "Gran doesn't charge anyone under the age of ten, even at the bakery. She loves kids, and she likes nothing better than spoiling them. My brothers and I are living proof of that."

"How many brothers do you have?" Aubrey asked, apparently over her initial shyness.

Hunkering down to her level, Emma said, "I have two, Sam and Brian, both older than me. Sometimes being the youngest is fun, and sometimes they bug me."

The childish phrasing puzzled Rick for a moment, until he saw his younger daughter nod in agreement. "Me, too."

"I don't bug you," Caitlin corrected her with a frown.

"Yes, you do, but it's okay. I still love you."

"Aww…" The older girl beamed at her little shadow and pulled her close for a sideways hug. "That's so sweet. I love you, too, Froggy."

Rick laughed out loud, and Emma looked up at him. "Froggy?"

"When we were waiting for Aubrey to join us, we let Caitlin name the baby. There was a character in a kids' movie at the time named Froggy, and she picked that. We thought it was cute, so we went along. After that, it became one of our inside family jokes."

"I'm very familiar with those," Emma commented, smiling as she stood.

"I've met your brothers, so I don't doubt that for a second."

While they finished off their snack, they chatted lightly about the weather and the upcoming spring concert and art show to be held at the school. While his daughters occupied themselves by rearranging Emma's dwindling stock by color, Rick noticed a stack of flyers sitting on her table. Recognizing her sister-in-law Lindsay's handiwork on the promotional material, he picked one up to see what it was about.

One-of-a-kind jewelry designed and handmade by Emma Calhoun. All proceeds to benefit the Liberty Creek After School Arts Program.

Amazed that she was giving up an entire Saturday and not keeping any of the money she made, he turned the sheet toward her. "I didn't realize you were doing this for nothing."

"Not for nothing," she corrected him sweetly. "For a bunch of awesome kids who enjoy art as much as I do."

"Is the program really in danger of being cut?"

"Always. It's open to students of every age, and they bus kids who want to participate down from the middle and high schools. It's a great alternative to them going home to an empty house, but every year the school budget gets tighter, and there's only so much money to go around. Last year we barely squeaked by."

"How many students use it?"

"That's not the point," she reminded him curtly, a flash of temper pinking her cheeks.

"Children deserve to have a creative outlet, and some of the older ones need a place to hang out after school. This program does both."

The scolding was delivered in the same soft voice she'd used before, but it seethed with a frustration that told him she'd delivered this speech many times before. Hoping to soothe her ruffled feelings, he smiled. "It sounds like a valuable thing to offer, and I didn't mean to imply otherwise. I was just curious about the numbers, because sometimes using them to illustrate your point carries more weight with bureaucrats than pure sentiment does."

"Well, that's different," she announced, shaking off the fit of temper with a breezy laugh. "I guess I'm so used to defending the arts, I get my back up too easily. Thirty-four kids come in on a regular basis, but around holidays like Christmas and Easter we get more because they like making gifts for people."

No mention of Mother's Day, he noticed, although he was fairly certain that was also on the list. He appreciated her avoiding the difficult subject, and while he didn't normally interfere in people's endeavors, her sensitivity made him more inclined to volunteer some advice. "If you'd like, we can sit down and review the finances for the program, see if there might be a way to generate the revenue you need to keep it on firmer footing. That way you and your Rembrandts-in-training wouldn't be so dependent on the school board to keep the club afloat."

She blinked up at him as if she didn't quite follow his train of thought. "Finances for the program?"

"How much is earmarked in the budget for supplies, your salary, things like that," he clarified as patiently as he could. Sarah had often accused him of assuming that everyone had his affinity for numbers and how certain strategies affected a company's bottom line, he mused sadly. Apparently, his approach to problem-solving still had some room for improvement.

"Oh, there's no salary involved," Emma told him, laughing as if it was absurd for him to think there might be. "I go into the budget hearing every May and beg, praying they'll find some money to help offset my expenses."

Rick couldn't believe what she was telling him. He'd never met anyone who so willingly sacrificed not only their free time but also a chunk of their own money to make sure kids had a fun place to go after school. From her answer, he realized that while the school contributed a share, it didn't fund the program entirely. That left Emma picking up the rest on a teacher's salary, which he suspected wasn't all that much in a small town like Liberty Creek.

"Maybe parents could pay a small fee to help defray the costs."

Emma firmly shook her head. "Folks around here have a tough enough time making ends meet as it is. I'm afraid if I ask for something like that, their kids won't be able to come anymore. That would leave some of them going home to an empty house after school, and I can't stand the thought of that."

"This isn't a big city," he argued sensibly. "It's not like they'll get into trouble with a gang or something like that."

"But it's lonely," she argued, compassion deepening the blue of her eyes in an emotion he could almost feel. "To my mind, that's just as bad for them. I'd rather put in a few extra hours of my time and give them a bright, constructive place to go hang out with their friends than know they're by themselves, plopped in front of the TV or some video game until their parents get home from work."

That was the challenge so many modern families faced, Rick knew. As he'd worked his way up the ladder from floor teller to bank management, he'd always known that he was fortunate to be in a business that had allowed Sarah to be a full-time mother, and now enabled him to afford a dedicated nanny and housekeeper. If he had to cope with day care and car pools on top of his demanding job, he wasn't sure how well it would go. But he was fairly certain that his girls wouldn't be nearly as secure and happy as they were now.

This was his first opportunity to work as an assistant branch manager, and he wanted to shine in the position. Not so much for himself, but for his sweet girls. While Patriots Bank was a collection of modestly sized regional offices, his boss and mentor had made it clear that his intention was to groom Rick for something more. That meant a spot at one of his larger banks that offered an equally larger salary. Then Caitlin and Aubrey would have a permanent home to grow up in rather than the time-worn rental near the square that he'd been forced to take.

Rick acknowledged that there was no way for him to replace their mother, but he'd do everything in his power to make certain his daughters never wanted for anything he could possibly give them.

"I get that," he relented, letting go of his

usual pragmatism to see things from Emma's vastly different point of view. "And I think it's great that you're willing to do it. I also think you deserve to be compensated for your time."

"There are more important things in life than money," she told him. Nodding toward his content daughters, she smiled up at him. "Being a father, you know that better than anyone."

It wasn't exactly a scolding, but her gentle reminder hit him harder than if she'd yelled at him for being a coldhearted, capitalistic jerk. He couldn't recall the last time that he'd paused in his busy schedule long enough to consider what was most important in his life.

Without question, his family came first. But during the past two years, while struggling to cope with the demands of his career and raising two precocious daughters on his own, he'd become more concerned about making it from day-to-day with no major disasters. He adored his girls, and he'd do everything humanly possible to keep them safe and happy in a world that seemed to grow more complicated every year.

In Emma's quiet conviction, he heard an echo of how he'd felt when he was a new father, overjoyed by the simple pleasures that had governed their time as a family. Coming home from the hospital, crawling, walking, first words—those memories were precious to him. All the more because Sarah had been part of them.

But, as Caitlin liked to remind him on a regular basis, they weren't babies anymore. At six and four, they were far from being independent, but they didn't need him for every little thing as they once did. His role in their lives was gradually changing and would continue to evolve until the day he died. His goal was to enjoy every moment of that time to the fullest, but sometimes he lost sight of what that meant.

It didn't escape him that this lovely artist had been the one to set him straight, and he couldn't come up with a better way to repay her than to help save the program she'd put so much effort into.

"You're right," he agreed, smiling to show her there were no hard feelings. "And I appreciate you pointing that out to me. In return, I'd like to support you at the upcoming board meeting. When is it?"

"This coming Wednesday night. But it's really not necessary for you to come. I know how busy you must be."

"Everyone is, but we all make time for the

things that matter. If you can stop by the bank tomorrow around three, I'll take a look at what you have and see if there's anything I can do to help you make your case for keeping the program a little stronger."

Emma gave him a long, assessing look, and he got the feeling she was sizing him up. Deciding if she could trust him, maybe. "That sounds good to me. Thank you."

She added a bright smile, and he found himself returning the gesture with no thought at all. He was no stranger to feminine attention, which was why he kept his wedding band firmly in place. Liberty Creek was a small town, and the last thing he needed was women thinking he was available. As a single dad, he'd gone through that before, and it had always ended badly. While he'd enjoy having someone to spend his scant free time with, he wasn't about to subject his young daughters— or himself—to the dating scene anytime soon.

So for now he'd keep his wedding ring on and avoid getting into a relationship that would probably end up going nowhere and making a lot of people miserable. It was just simpler that way.

Chapter Two

"You really don't have to do this," Emma protested while the Marshalls helped her dismantle her display area. She'd sold most of her stock, and while she wasn't sure of the final tally in her cash box, she could tell from the weight of it that between sales and donations, she'd done well. "The boys will be coming over to help me when they're done working for the day."

"We're here now, so we can save them a trip. It's really not a problem," Rick assured her, setting out some white cushioned boxes for Caitlin and Aubrey to load her extra jewelry into. "Make sure you don't tangle the chains on those necklaces, Cait. Knots are no fun."

"My hair got all tangled last week," she commented with a sour face. "It took Mrs. Fields a long time to get it out."

"I like braids," Aubrey informed Emma, holding one out to prove her point.

She was so adorable, Emma couldn't help laughing. "So do I, especially ones as pretty as yours. Who does them up so nicely for you?"

"Daddy. He's good at lots of things."

"Like what?"

"Making waffles, doing Band-Aids, singing," Aubrey replied, ticking off his admirable skills on her pudgy fingers. "Mostly, he's good at being Daddy."

From the corner of her eye, Emma saw him smile while he broke down the table that had held the handmade items she'd been selling. He didn't say anything, but his expression told her that his daughter's praise meant a lot to him. From their conversation earlier about him being a numbers guy, she'd gotten the impression that he was the pragmatic type who didn't get overly sentimental about things.

Seeing this softer side of him made her wonder if she'd misjudged the young widower. Timid by nature, she certainly could relate to why some people chose to keep their feelings under wraps. Considering his profession, he'd probably learned that it was smart to bide his time and carefully assess new situations—and acquaintances—before jumping in with both feet.

Emma's own experience with the uncertainties of life had taught her to embrace each day and squeeze every ounce of joy from it that was humanly possible. It was tiring sometimes, especially because her health still tended to ebb and flow without much warning. But during all those months of chemo and her challenging recovery, she'd promised herself one thing.

When God finally decided to call her home, she'd go with a peaceful heart, secure in the knowledge that she'd used all the talents He'd given her and had accomplished everything she could have done during her time on earth.

After closing the back door of her hatchback, she turned to her assistants and gave them a smile. "Thanks so much for all your help today. What have you got planned for the rest of this weekend?"

Alternating, the girls rattled off their lists of what they hoped to achieve, including cleaning their room, finishing the puzzle they'd been working on and learning how to make snickerdoodles.

"Why snickerdoodles?" she asked.

"They're Daddy's favorite," Caitlin informed her in a tone that implied the reason should have been obvious to Emma. She nearly laughed, but didn't want to insult the bright girl by giving the impression that she wasn't taking the subject seriously.

Instead, she sighed. "That all sounds like a lot of fun. I'll be doing dishes and laundry, which isn't nearly as interesting."

"But very important," Rick said, giving his darling girls a father-knows-best kind of look. "Work first, right, ladies?"

"Yes, then cookies," Aubrey agreed, braids bobbing with enthusiasm for the treat that awaited them at the end of the job.

This time Emma couldn't hold back her laughter, and after a moment he joined her. He'd struck her as a very serious man, and now that she was more familiar with what he had to manage on a daily basis, she completely understood his reserved demeanor. Still, she couldn't help noticing that his eyes twinkled when he smiled at either of his daughters. It told her that there was a lighter side to his personality, and she hoped that he might feel more comfortable showing it to people as he got to know them better.

Not to her, of course. She was Caitlin's teacher, which meant considering anything serious with Rick Marshall would be foolish, at best. Beyond that, between her job and ongoing recovery, she had more than enough to handle as it was. Some days she woke up so drained, she could barely drag herself out of bed to face the day ahead of her. The Marshalls had already been through that heart-wrenching territory with Sarah, and she'd never dream of encouraging any sort of relationship that might lead to their family being forced to re-trace those agonizing steps.

It was one thing to be optimistic about her condition for her own sake. It was quite an-other to pull someone else into the uncertainty she faced every day. While she'd love to have a family of her own one day, she'd come to terms with the fact that, at least for a while, she was better off staying single. It was lonely sometimes, but in her heart, she knew it was for the best.

"Before we do any of that," he said as he fished his car keys from the pocket of his shorts, "we'll go over to Miss Calhoun's and help put all of her supplies away."

"That's really not necessary," she objected. "You've spent most of the afternoon here, and I'd hate to keep you from your fun any longer."

He didn't respond to that as he beeped open the doors of a gray sedan so the girls could climb into their spots in the backseat. Glancing at them, he then turned to Emma. "I know you're not supposed to say this kind of thing to a lady, but you look totally wiped out. I can't just take off and leave you here to manage all this stuff by yourself."

It hadn't occurred to her that he'd be able to read her physical signs so well, and then she reminded herself that he was all too familiar with the kind of exhaustion that occasionally still came out of nowhere to stop her in her tracks. So, since he clearly had no intention of letting the subject drop, she relented with a smile. "That's very sweet of you. Thanks."

"Not a problem."

His quick smile seemed genuine enough, but she noticed that it didn't quite reach his eyes. So much sadness, she lamented as she got into her car and started the engine. Sarah Marshall must have been a remarkable woman for him to still love her so much even though she was gone. That kind of loyalty was rare these days, which Emma knew from personal experience. Her last boyfriend had bolted soon after her cancer diagnosis, and while she didn't blame him, his lack of fortitude had been a tremendous disappointment to her. That Rick had remained strong for his family said a lot about the kind of man he was beneath the expertly pressed shorts and deck shoes.

When they arrived at her house, she pulled into the driveway far enough to allow Rick to park behind her. She got out and looked back to find that there was a ruckus going on in his backseat. She peeked in to find the girls bouncing in place, pointing at the old maple tree that shaded the front yard. She walked back to meet her guests, and he chuckled as Caitlin and Aubrey bolted from the car and made a beeline for the tree. "I think they like your swing."

"So do I," she replied, strolling over to join them. The seat was wide enough for them to sit side by side, and she gave them a light push to get them started. "My brothers and I grew up here, and my dad hung a swing from this tree when we were kids. There have been a few more since then, and the last time it needed to be replaced I almost didn't bother. Sam insisted on hanging a new one for me, to keep the tradition going. Seeing how much your girls like it, I'm glad he did."

"You've always lived here?" Caitlin asked, clearly amazed by the concept.

"Yes. I went away for college, and when I was done, the elementary school's art teacher was ready to retire. She encouraged me to pursue art when I was young, so it just seemed right to come back here and pick up where she'd left off."

"That's so awesome," the girl approved, glancing at the house and then staring up into the wide branches overhead with a huge grin. "I would've done that, too."

Emma was happy with her decision, but she had to admit that sometimes she wondered what she'd missed by so quickly returning to her tiny hometown. "Oh, I'm sure you'll have lots of adventures when you're older. There's a big, exciting world out there for you to explore."

"I guess. But it'd be nice to have a house like this to come back to."

"Did someone paint your windows?" Aubrey asked.

Emma laughed. "Sort of. They're called stained glass, and it takes a real artist to do them right. My cousin Jordan makes them, and he did them for me as a housewarming gift when I bought the house from my parents a few years ago."

"Was your house cold?" the adorable cherub asked, forehead puckering in obvious confusion.

At first Emma didn't understand the question. Then she replayed their exchange in her head and smiled. "A housewarming is when you invite people to see your new home and they bring you presents of things you might need. Like towels or a welcome mat, things like that."

"And your cousin brought you windows that he made special for you?" When Emma nodded, Aubrey's eyes widened in appreciation. "That was really nice of him."

"Yes, it was."

"Is he your favorite cousin?" Emma nodded again, and the girl said, "My favorite cousin is Gigi. She lives in Vi-ginia. We used to live in Charleston by Grammy and Grampa, but then Daddy got a new job and we moved here."

Emma glanced over at Rick, who was leaning against the tree, listening to their conversation. When she caught his eye, he gave her a what-can-you-do sort of look, but he didn't step in to cut off his suddenly chatty daughter. So many people did that to young children, and Emma was pleased to discover that he wasn't one of them. Kids were openly curious about everything around them, and she'd always hated it when adults tried to maneuver them into behaving more properly.

Quite honestly, she believed that if grown-ups could find a way to be as open-minded as kids were, life would be a lot more fun for everyone.

"And I'm very glad he did," she told them as she went up the front porch steps of the vintage Craftsman house. "We can always use someone like your dad around here. In Liberty Creek," she added quickly, to avoid any potential misunderstanding. The Marshall girls were sweet and engaging, but she was well aware that children often repeated things they'd heard without realizing how they might be received when heard out of context. She didn't want Rick—or anyone else—getting the idea that she personally liked having him around. Considering the Liberty Creek gossip mill, that was the last thing either of them needed.

Pushing open the beautiful original door that Sam had recently refinished for her, she stepped into the living room and motioned them inside. "Come on in."

The girls pushed past their father and stopped so abruptly, he nearly ran them over. When he'd regained his balance, he looked around with the same awed expression they were wearing.

"Wow," he murmured, clearly trying to take

everything in at once. "This is not at all what I was expecting."

"I don't have much use for a living room," she explained. "What I needed was a studio."

"And I'd say you have one. This is incredible. Don't touch anything, girls."

"Oh, they're fine," Emma assured him. "Everything's dry, and there's nothing breakable in here. You caught me on a good day—I just cleaned."

Eyes sparkling in appreciation, Caitlin slowly made her way between easels, pausing to stare at the panoramic landscape that was almost finished. It was so large, it spanned two easels all by itself. Looking up at Emma, she asked, "Is this the town?"

"You have a good eye," Emma praised her student with a smile. Taking down an aging tintype that was tacked to the upper edge of the canvas, she handed it to Caitlin. "It's Liberty Creek, but this is how it looked a long time ago. Back when people drove horses and wagons instead of cars, and my grandmother's bakery was a general store that sold things like fabric, candy, hammers and saddles."

Rick sauntered over and looked above their heads at the scene. "This is what Liberty Creek Forge looked like back in its heyday?"

"More or less. This piece is a surprise for Brian and Lindsay, so please don't mention it to either of them. I thought it might look nice hanging in the lobby at the forge."

"Nice?" he echoed with a chuckle. "I'd say it'll be the centerpiece. The detail is incredible, right down to the dog sitting on the front landing. It looks just like their Riley, Aussie markings and all. It doesn't seem like I'm looking at a portrait of something two-dimensional. You have a knack for making it feel like I actually went back in time and am standing right there."

Emma had been sketching, painting and sculpting her entire life. It was something she'd always done, because she couldn't *not* do it. People often admired her work, but to most she was the school's art teacher. Or Sam and Brian's little sister, or Ellie's youngest grandchild. It was one of the drawbacks of never having left home, she supposed. People saw her as the starry-eyed pixie she'd always been, not the capable woman she'd become.

She wasn't one to cater to her ego, but Rick's assessment of her talent made her stand up a little straighter, proud to share her work with him.

There were several large frames standing on edge against one wall, and he slowly flipped through them, asking questions about her inspiration for each. One in particular appeared to interest him, and he pulled it free to set it out on its own. To her utter astonishment, he looked over at her and asked, "Is this for sale?"

"For sale?" she squeaked, totally flabbergasted by the idea of it. "You mean, you want to buy it from me?"

"If you're willing to part with it, then yes. My office at the bank is about the blandest place you've ever seen, and I've been hunting for artwork to bring in some color. This autumn forest scene would be perfect."

"It would?" Realizing she sounded like a complete moron, Emma scraped up some dignity and tried to sound more professional. "I'm pleased that you like it so much."

"How much is it?"

She'd never sold anything this large before. Mostly, the oversize canvases were gifts for family and friends. Or they wound up hanging on her own walls until she ran out of space and carefully wrapped them in brown paper before consigning them to the attic. Completely out of her depth, she fell back on a tactic that she'd learned from her late grandfather when he used to sell his handmade metal items at the area's many summertime crafts shows. "That depends. How much do you think it's worth?"

Rick tilted his head in a chiding gesture. "You're not exactly a hardheaded business-woman, are you?"

"Not many dreamers are," she informed him, smarting a bit from the dig.

Judging by the sudden shift in his features, he'd picked up on her annoyance. "I'm sorry. I didn't mean to insult you. As far as I'm concerned, your approach is a refreshing change from the money-first people I deal with every day."

"Oh. Well, then, apology accepted."

When she named a price that seemed reasonable to her, he shook his head. "You're selling yourself way too short. A one-of-a-kind piece this size, of this quality, is worth twice that much at any art gallery in New England."

Emma's jaw fell open in astonishment. "Seriously? I had no idea."

"I can see that," he commented, adding a smile that made her feel slightly less naive. Setting the frame carefully against the wall, he pulled out his wallet and fingered through the contents before handing her several bills. "Will this be enough to hold it until I can come back with the rest and pick it up?"

It was more money than she'd ever made in an afternoon, and she tried not to stammer. "Of course. Would you like to have it framed?"

"You do that, too?"

"Well, Sam makes them custom for me. He's the carpenter in the family."

"That's right—I've seen his craftsmanship over at the forge. When I was admiring the repaired vintage woodwork he recently installed there, Brian told me that there's nothing Sam can't build or fix."

Her oldest brother had been through a lot since leaving the army, and Rick's admiration of his skills made her smile. "Very true. If you get in touch with him and tell him what style of frame you'd like, I'm sure he'd be happy to take care of it for you."

"Sounds good." Flashing her a quick smile, he said, "Girls, let's help Miss Calhoun unload her car and then head home. We've still got things to get done today."

In a matter of minutes, all of her crafts show supplies were stowed in the enclosed side porch she'd converted into her storage space, and she was waving goodbye to the Marshalls. When she was alone, she strolled into the living room and stared thoughtfully at the large painting she'd somehow managed to sell without even trying. A teacher's salary didn't go very far when you were maintaining your own house and still paying off a car and college loans, so the extra cash would be a welcome addition to her modest bank account.

This month it would be easier to pay her bills, and she might even be able to put a little bit away for a future rainy day. They always seemed to pop up at the worst times, like when the aging chimney had started leaking into the living room and needed repair in the middle of a frigid, snowy January.

Glancing up, she smiled. "I'm not sure why You did that, but thank You."

Emma was late.

Rick checked his watch again, confirming that it was now ten after three and he was still waiting for her. When she'd expressed concern about interrupting his afternoon, he'd assumed that meant she valued his time. It had made it easier for him to be more generous than he might have been otherwise.

But now he was regretting the uncharacteristic lapse in his clockwork-style routine. Business school had taught him the importance of efficiently using every minute of the day to benefit whichever company he was working for. Having spent the past six years climbing the ladder through the banking industry, he knew that at least part of his success was due to his unyielding discipline.

But there was something about Emma Calhoun that made him want to step outside his regimen and be more spontaneous. That unnamed quality had nudged him to cast aside his family's usual Saturday routine and follow her to the quirky home filled with a creative light that he still remembered vividly. While his daughters enjoyed their tumbling array of collectibles and stuffed animals, in his own room he preferred clean, simple lines and as little clutter as possible. He attributed the difference to their younger view of the world around them, but maybe there was more to it than that.

Quarter after, he noticed while he checked into his email to avoid feeling as if he was wasting his afternoon. It wasn't like the lovely art teacher had asked him to bend the rules for her, he reminded himself wryly. He'd done it willingly, and all on his own. Lesson learned.

"Rick, I'm so sorry," the lady in question apologized as she lunged through the door into his office, loaded down with an armful of manila folders. "There was an art emergency at school, and I totally forgot to call you to let you know I was running late."

That was a new one, he thought as he shook off his irritation and stood to motion her to one of the client chairs opposite his desk. "What's an art emergency?"

"One of my middle schoolers was making a model of Independence Hall and accidentally glued his fingers together. I know, I know," she added, holding up one hand in a quieting gesture. "It's crazy, and I didn't believe him at first, either. But when I realized he was serious, I knew I couldn't send him home like that. Once I stopped laughing, it took me a good ten minutes to get him unstuck and cleaned up."

Her charming account chased away the last of his annoyance, and he chuckled. "Boys, huh?"

"And how. If you knew half the scrapes my brothers got into when we were growing up, you'd never believe they survived."

"Meaning you were the perfect child?" The question sounded perilously close to teasing, which was completely inappropriate given the professional setting they were in, and he gave himself a mental shake. In his defense, it was hard to remain detached from someone as bubbly as Emma Calhoun.

"The most perfect one," she informed him, mischief twinkling in those crystal-blue eyes. "Just ask my dad."

Rick had encountered Steve Calhoun a couple of times and had no doubt that the burly mechanic had been wrapped around Emma's little finger since the time she was old enough to smile at him. Warm and open, she'd quickly broken through Rick's usual reserve, and he was an expert at keeping his distance. Being the father of two charmers himself, he could only imagine how completely Steve doted on his only daughter.

Eager to move the conversation onto safer footing, he glanced down at the folders she'd dumped onto his formerly empty leather blotter. "So, what have you got here?"

"Ideas for projects, sketches, wish lists from the kids, things like that. You said to bring everything related to the after-school program."

"When I said everything, I meant all your receipts and invoices," he explained patiently. He thought he'd been perfectly clear about what he needed, but apparently they had a difference of opinion on what was important.

"Oh, I have those, too."

Opening one of the unmarked folders, she finger-walked through the pages inside, plucking out a receipt here and there. After about a minute of that he honestly thought he was about to lose his mind. "They're all mixed in, then?"

"Well, yes," she replied as if she had no idea that there was a better way to organize her materials. "I keep them connected to the project idea they belong with. That way I know how many kids wanted to do each one, and how much I spent on supplies to get them done."

Rick grudgingly admitted that her system did make sense. In a convoluted, totally random kind of way. Her free-spirited demeanor reminded him of his daughters, and it occurred to him that the best strategy for getting through this task was to recognize that their minds worked in different ways. Once he accepted that, he could figure out how to meld their vastly dissimilar talents into a cohesive approach.

He could take a shot at it, anyway. Fortunately for him, he liked taking on a new challenge once in a while. It helped to keep his problem-solving chops in shape.

"Tell you what," he suggested, tapping the stack of folders. "Why don't we go through these together, sorting and categorizing your records into something that we can present to the board on Wednesday?"

Her forehead puckered in confusion. "I thought we were going to do that now."

"I didn't realize how big a job it was," he confided, feeling more than a little foolish about admitting that to her. "I have a meeting at four, but tomorrow afternoon is clear and we won't be rushed to get it done."

For some reason she hesitated. After a moment she said, "That's very nice, but tomorrow afternoon is supposed to be beautiful. I hate to intrude on time you could be spending with Caitlin and Aubrey."

Quite honestly, it had never occurred to him that with his schedule clear after one o'clock tomorrow, he could leave the bank and hang out with his girls either in their spacious backyard or at the town playground. His father had instilled in him the importance of always striving for more, working harder than his peers to ensure that his achievements shone the brightest. In any business, having happy customers translated to success, which brought you more income and security for the future. But now that this soft-spoken teacher had pointed out another way for him to use his free afternoon, Rick saw no reason not to take advantage of it.

"I'll do that," he agreed with a smile, "and then you can come by my house around five tomorrow after the arts program is over. We'll be back from the park by then, and I know the girls would love to see you."

"What a fabulous idea!" Emma approved, eyes sparkling with a childlike enthusiasm that even a pragmatic data hound like him could appreciate. "Maybe they'd like to help me pick out which projects I should include in the slides. I usually do that to show the board some real-life examples of our results and the benefit the kids get from working on their projects."

She'd called herself a dreamer the other day, and he was pleasantly surprised to discover that she had a practical streak under all that perky sweetness. "That's a nice touch, for sure. With the fate of the arts program on the line, this presentation is important to you and a lot of other people here in town. If we both put our minds to it, we'll have a better chance of getting your proposal approved."

She studied him for a few moments before asking, "What about you?"

"I'm sorry?"

"You made it sound like the program's not important to you. If that's the case, I don't understand why you'd go to all this trouble to save it."

"I'm a numbers guy," he explained, leaning back in his chair to put a little more distance between them. "But intellectually, I understand the value of creative things."

"You liked that landscape painting well enough to pay me a lot of money for it," she pointed out, clearly baffled by his response. "Or were you just being nice to Caitlin's new teacher?"

In spite of his resolve to treat her professionally, he smiled as he shook his head. "No, I really do like it. As you can see, this office needs something."

"It needs a lot of somethings," she corrected him with a cheeky grin. "All these empty beige walls... This must be what the inside of oatmeal looks like."

Her comment made him laugh out loud, and through his open door he saw a couple of the other managers stop and stare at him. Their amazed expressions told him they didn't know he had a sense of humor, and in fairness, he hadn't given them much reason to think otherwise. As far as his coworkers knew, he was a serious, nose-to-the-grindstone kind of person who worked hard and always got the job done flawlessly and ahead of schedule.

Now that he thought about it, he seldom laughed unless he was with his girls. Why that had suddenly changed was beyond him, but he couldn't deny that his lovely guest had something to do with it. Although the easing of his usual composure felt good to him, he recognized that the effect would by necessity be short-lived.

Once he was finished with the task he'd volunteered for, he and Emma would return to the uncomplicated relationship they'd had since he'd moved to Liberty Creek. She was his daughter's teacher, and he was her brother's banker. Simple, straightforward and pleasant.

The realization should have been comforting to him. But as he helped her scoop up the documents she'd brought with her, there was a sinking feeling in his chest. It only got worse as he walked her to the bank's main entrance door and said goodbye.

Back in his office, he sensed that something had changed. It took him a minute, but then he registered the fact that the perfume she wore had lingered behind her, lacing the air with the scent of a summertime garden. The idea of sharing a picnic in the town's charming gazebo with her flashed into his head.

At this point in his life, a romantic connection was the furthest thing from his mind, he thought as he resolutely got back to work.

Allowing himself to fall into a relationship with another woman battling cancer was simply out of the question. After two years of unimaginable heartache, he and his daughters had finally begun to recover from losing Sarah. He had no intention of setting them on that path again.

Resilient as they were, he wasn't sure they'd make it through a second time.

Chapter Three

"**M**iss Calhoun is here!" Caitlin sang, sailing down the colonial home's handcrafted wooden staircase and out the front door before Rick had a chance to respond.

Clearly amused, Mrs. Fields turned and gave him an indulgent smile. "She really loves her new teacher, doesn't she?"

"Cait's my little Rembrandt," he said fondly, reaching out to where Aubrey sat at the kitchen table to flip the complex single French braid he'd finally mastered with a little help from an internet discussion board for dads who needed advice on such things. "Aubrey's going to be a scientist. Right, honey?"

Munching her apple, she tilted her head with a serious expression. "Or a zookeeper. Or maybe a really good cook, like Mrs. Fields."

The grandmotherly woman laughed and hugged her from behind. "Whatever you decide, I'm sure you'll be the best. I'm just glad to know that girls these days have so many choices of what they want to do for a career. In my day, there weren't nearly as many options."

Fascinated, Aubrey spun partway around in her chair. "What did you want to be?"

"Oh, it wasn't very realistic," the woman responded, waving her hand as if her old dream was something that should be pushed aside and forgotten.

Ordinarily, Rick took people at their word and didn't pry beneath the surface of what they said to him. For some reason this time he went the other way. "Maybe not, but it sounds like it meant something to you when you were younger. What was it?"

After a moment she shook her head with a wistful look. "I wanted to be a music teacher. I love children, and helping them learn new things makes me happy."

That explained why she was so wonderful with his girls, Rick thought in admiration. He'd never asked the agency for details on prospective nannies beyond the usual references and salary requirements. It occurred to him that as he'd gotten to know more about her over the past few months, he'd begun to view the cheerful middle-aged woman as more than an employee.

She felt like part of the family. How had that happened? he wondered. Before he had a chance to ponder it, Caitlin joined them in the kitchen, pulling a laughing Emma behind her.

"Miss Calhoun said we can call her Emma when we're away from school. Isn't that awesome, Daddy?"

"Very awesome," he agreed, chuckling as he stood to relieve their visitor of the load she was carrying. Glancing inside the large plastic bin labeled "Art Program," he looked at her in confusion. "There's a lot more in here than what you brought to the bank yesterday."

"More of the kids' artwork," she explained before dropping into the chair next to Aubrey. Peering at the preschooler's book of animals, she pointed to one of the pictures. "I've never seen one of these before. What is it?"

Always ready to jump in, Caitlin quickly said, "It's a—"

Rick cut her off with a shake of his head, and she abruptly fell silent to let her younger sister answer. Aubrey was a little slower to warm up to adults, and he looked for any opportunity to encourage her to interact with people outside her very limited circle.

To his surprise she quietly confided, "I don't know."

"Me, neither," Emma said easily, sliding a little closer. "Why don't we go through the letters in its name together and see if we can figure out what they spell?"

"Okay." Aubrey's small index finger moved from one letter to the next as she recited the letters. If she got stuck, she glanced at Emma, who filled in the alphabetical blank. When they were done, they sounded out the name together, and she sat back with a triumphant grin. "Coatimundi. It's really cute."

"Well, how about that?" Emma said, giving her a quick hug. "Thanks to you, now I know what they look like, and that they live in Mexico."

"And how to spell it," Caitlin added, patting her sister's head. "Great job, Froggy."

She sat down on the other side of Emma, and the three of them leafed through the book, stopping here and there for a closer look at whatever snagged their attention. Seeing Emma with his daughters did something strange to Rick's heart. He'd grown so accustomed to them being a three-person family that he didn't often consider what they might be missing out on. He adored them—would lay down his life for theirs without a single thought if it came to that. Their past nannies had been wonderful, and Mrs. Fields brought a steady, compassionate demeanor into their household that he really appreciated.

But he couldn't deny that his girls needed something more than he could give them, even though he could afford the best caretakers in the area. Even when Sarah's own health was failing, she'd remained an unwavering presence in their young lives, calm and comforting until the end. That was a mother's love, he realized. And no matter how hard he tried, he simply couldn't give them that.

But Emma had an undeniable way with them, and it wasn't the first time he'd noticed it. Maybe it was because she worked with kids all day and obviously enjoyed being around them. Or maybe she'd formed a bond with Caitlin because of her illness, and Aubrey followed along because she adored her big sister and frequently copied her behavior.

Or maybe that was simply the kind of person Emma was. In his experience, kind, caring strangers were so rare that he could quickly count them on one hand. Having met Emma

Calhoun, he had to allow for the possibility that he'd stumbled across another one. If that was the case, he was beginning to get the feeling that they'd all be better off for knowing her.

"Mr. Marshall," Mrs. Fields interrupted his thoughts in her usual brisk way. "There's a lasagna in the oven, and it will be ready in about fifteen minutes. If you're set for tonight, I'll head home and let you enjoy your evening."

"I knew I smelled something delicious when I walked in earlier," he commented.

"Well, it's Tuesday, and that's lasagna night. Girls, go wash up so you're ready when your dinner is."

Caitlin and Aubrey scrambled for the powder room, and Rick walked their nanny out the way he did every day. After wishing her a good night, he slid the dead bolt and returned to his guest.

When he came back into the kitchen, Emma gave him a curious look, and he chuckled. "Okay, you got me. The girls like lasagna and I'm a creature of habit."

"You don't have to explain anything to me," she pointed out gently. "This is your house, and you can have whatever you want for dinner."

He knew that, but something had prompted him to clarify their routine for her. It was none of her business, as she'd told him, but he didn't want her thinking that he was some kind of rigid financial type with no imagination. Why her opinion mattered to him, he couldn't say, but it did.

"I didn't mean to interrupt your dinner," she went on, heading for the back door. "When you're finished, just give me a call and I'll come back."

"Would you like to join us?" he blurted without thinking. That was unusual for him, a guy who normally considered every angle of a situation before deciding how to respond. But this sweet, soft-spoken artist had gotten to him on a level he didn't quite understand, and he was definitely off his game.

"Are you sure? I mean, this is family time for you."

"Oh, please stay, Emma!" Caitlin begged, tugging one of her hands while Aubrey latched onto the other. "Daddy told us about your project, and I want to help."

"Me, too," Aubrey chimed in. "But I'm not allowed to use the big scissors. They're too sharp."

"Then we'll find you some smaller ones," Emma assured her, leaning down to pull them into an adorable group hug. "It's a big job, and your daddy and I can use all the hands we can get."

"That's settled, then," Rick announced just as the oven timer rang. Stepping back, he motioned them into the dining room, where the table was neatly set for three. "Ladies, if you'll make yourselves comfortable, I'll bring in our dinner."

"And an extra plate for Emma," Caitlin reminded him in a tone that was far too grown up for his taste. He had a feeling that before he could blink, his six-year-old would be sixteen and he'd be meeting her potential boyfriends at the door, casually holding his nine-iron in a not-so-subtle warning.

"Yes, ma'am," he agreed, swallowing a laugh as he got to work.

The three of them normally occupied half of the round cherry dining table so they could more easily talk and pass the dishes. To accommodate their visitor, they sat more evenly spaced, chatting about their days as if the four of them ate together every night. To anyone out on the sidewalk passing by the large bay window, they'd look like any other family sharing a meal at the end of the day. It struck him again that while he'd taken over Sarah's care of the girls, he couldn't ever take her place.

Not that he hadn't tried, he mused with a frown. It just wasn't possible.

"Daddy?"

Aubrey's voice dragged him back to their dinner, and he looked over at her. "Yes?"

"You look sad."

"I'm fine, baby," he assured her, forcing a smile. "How's your lasagna?"

"Yummy. Mrs. Fields let me help her put the noodles in the pan. They were all slippery, and she let me eat some of the broken ones. It was fun."

"Aw, I wish I could've done that," Caitlin complained.

"You were at school, working on your painting with me," Emma reminded her. "You had your fun, and Aubrey had hers. That makes a nice day for everyone."

"Yeah, I guess. I just wish I could've done both."

"I know, but we can't be in two places at once," Emma said with an understanding smile. "Some other time, Aubrey can be the artist and you can be the cook."

Caitlin absorbed that and nodded. "Okay. That sounds good."

The young teacher's quick defusing of a potentially difficult situation was impressive, to say the least. "Emma, do you work for the UN in your spare time?"

Tilting her head, she gave him a quizzical look. "I'm sorry?"

"That was very diplomatic of you. I had no idea you were such a good mediator."

"Oh, that's nothing." She laughed, waving away the compliment. "Try negotiating a truce between two kindergarteners who both want to use the same purple crayon. *That's* a challenge." Beaming from one of his daughters to the other, she added, "You two are wonderful by comparison."

Rick thought so. But to hear that kind of comment from someone who'd witnessed them at less than their best behavior was comforting. He often worried that his hectic schedule prompted him to be too lenient with them as a way to make up for the hours that he was away from home. It was nice to know that Emma didn't see it that way.

After dinner they each took responsibility for a part of the cleaning-up process. There was a lot of laughter and teasing, especially when Aubrey's hair ribbon somehow found its way into the dishwasher. Once the kitchen was back to its usual state, Emma brought her tote in from the kitchen and set in on the dining room table. Rick fetched his laptop, and after a bit of wrangling around the girls, they all got to work.

"How about this one?" Caitlin asked Emma, showing her a picture a first-grader had sketched of her new kitten.

"Hmm…" Emma responded, tilting it toward Aubrey. "What do you think?"

Clearly pleased to be included in such a grown-up endeavor, his youngest studied it closely before declaring, "It's nice. I like cats."

"I like dogs," Caitlin said.

"I like both," Emma told them, spreading the artwork out so they could see it better. "Let's see if we can find a puppy picture in here somewhere, to balance it out. That way people who prefer one or the other will be happy."

Rick tapped away on his computer, glancing up now and then to see how things were going in the art department. He'd done so many presentations, he could probably compose them in his sleep by now. This one was about as simple as it got, so he was able to look busy while he kept an eye on the ladies' progress.

Usually, the girls clamped on to him the moment he got home and didn't let go until bedtime. Tonight they seemed perfectly content with Emma's attention, and it was interesting to watch them interact with her in such a warm, easygoing way. She was calm by nature, and she treated them more like short adults who deserved respect than like children to be coddled. He liked that.

More than that, he realized suddenly, he liked her. Emma's kindness and generosity had swept effortlessly through his little family, bringing them a friend at a time when they desperately needed one.

She'd been so good to them, and now he knew that helping her save the art program that was so dear to her was the ideal way to thank her. So he put his head down and got to work.

Emma had never been so nervous in her life. Not even her first day of student teaching had caused her this much stress, and she was at a loss to explain why. Waiting on the front landing of the high school for Rick, she reminded herself that she'd handled evenings like this before all by herself and they'd gone perfectly fine. She'd started attending the board meetings a couple of years ago when she'd first pitched her idea of transforming her impromptu art club into a bona fide after-school program, free of charge for any student who wanted to come. Some of the high schoolers who came in functioned as her assistants, helping the younger ones when they needed attention and she was occupied elsewhere. She suspected that the mentor role benefited the older students as much as the younger ones, and it was rewarding for her to know that she'd had a hand in helping these talented young people grow.

As promised, Rick's sedan pulled into the parking lot fifteen minutes before seven, and some of her anxiety receded. Because of his coaching and encouragement, she was confident that the concise, logical presentation they'd prepared was top-notch. It was her delivery she wasn't so sure of, but she swallowed her fear and plastered a smile on her face as she went to meet him.

"I'm so glad you're here," she blurted, cringing at the desperate note in her voice. She sounded like a teenager dreading a speech she had to make for English class rather than a competent adult. "I'm sorry—I guess I'm more on edge than I realized."

"Totally understandable," he assured her with a smile that looked as if he'd practiced it in a mirror. "This program is important to you, and it's natural to be a little anxious about tonight. That's why we put so much effort into refining the bullet points you're going to present to the board. Remember?"

"Yes, but you left the slides of the kids' projects mixed in, right? I think those are just as important as proving the monetary value of them having access to an extra art class."

"Of course I did," he said, patting his laptop case as if to prove to her that he hadn't forgotten anything. "This is your show, Emma. I'm just your support staff."

"I'm not used to having staff," she confided. "I kind of like it."

She also liked that he'd finally started calling her by her first name. Maybe just a little too much, she mused, concerned about their brief alliance becoming more than she was prepared to fend off. Now that she knew he was single, it definitely put a different spin on things.

Silently chiding herself for worrying about nothing, she pushed the bizarre reaction to him aside and led him into the school.

As they took their seats in the classroom where the meeting was taking place, he said, "I've enjoyed helping out. Tomorrow I have to go back to my oatmeal office and catch up on paperwork."

Her smile told him that she recognized her own description of his work space from the afternoon they'd first started working on this project.

"I like my paperwork better," she said, tapping the watercolor sketch of her class that adorned the front of her very organized new binder.

He gave her a long look, then leaned closer. "Don't repeat this to anyone at the bank, but so do I."

"Don't worry," she replied with a grin. "I won't tell a soul."

"No one would believe it, anyway."

There was a dejected quality to his normally mellow voice, and she frowned. "Why not?"

"I'm a numbers guy, remember?"

"You don't have to be *just* a numbers guy," she pointed out. "You could do something creative as a hobby."

Chuckling, he shook his head. "What's a hobby?"

"Something you do for fun." When she realized he'd simply been making a point about how hectic his life was, she felt silly for answering him that way. "What do you do for fun?"

"The girls are my fun. Without them—" He

shrugged as if he honestly didn't know what he'd do without Caitlin and Aubrey to break up his work routine.

"So you wouldn't go to a crafts show on your own?"

"No."

His voice had taken on a sudden strained quality, and she wondered what she'd done to bring on such a terse response. He seemed to appreciate her artwork, so it wasn't that he had no interest in that sort of thing. Then it hit her, and she realized that Sarah must have been the creative influence on their daughters.

Emma tried desperately to come up with something to say, but nothing seemed appropriate for someone she barely knew. And especially not surrounded by people who might overhear their conversation. So she decided the best option was to change the subject. "Could you tell me again how to run the slide show?"

"Sure." Opening the sleek laptop he'd brought with him, he took a cable from his bag and clicked to start the program. "Plug this into the console up front and it will connect the computer to the projector. Hit the enter key when you want to move ahead, and it will keep pace with you. That way you control the speed of it so you have time to answer any questions that come up while you're talking."

The mere idea of fielding unexpected inquiries made her queasy. "Do you really think they're going to ask me anything?"

"I have no idea, but I've learned that it's always better to be prepared in case they do."

"Okay." Taking a deep breath, she cast a worried glance around at the room that was much fuller now than it had been when she arrived. She recognized most of the attendees, which gave her a little boost of confidence. "I know almost everyone here. That should help."

"That's the spirit. You handle dozens of kids every day, which I think is much harder than giving a ten-minute talk. I'm sure you'll do fine."

Everyone has their talents, Emma mused, flattered that he seemed to value hers so highly. Many people assumed that working with kids was like playtime, and it was nice to know he respected how challenging her job could be.

Fortunately for her, she was the first agenda item after the usual greeting and the vote to accept the minutes from last month's session. So she gathered her courage, picked up Rick's laptop and went to the front of the room.

Glancing out into the audience, she found

his steady gaze, and he gave her a subtle nod of encouragement. That small gesture helped her immensely, and she faced the school board with a smile.

"Good evening, and thank you for letting me come in to speak to you." Shifting her view from them to the assembly, she went on, "Since you can read the agenda on the whiteboard, you all know why I'm here. Unless there are questions, I'll get started."

No one asked her anything, but a couple of the board members traded quizzical looks. Instinct told her something was up, but it wasn't her place to address them, so she put aside her misgivings and cued up the slides that Rick had helped her create. One covered the reasonable cost of the program compared with other after-school activities in the surrounding area. Another detailed the loose curriculum that governed the sessions, to show that it provided the kids with more than pure entertainment.

Finally, she reached the slides that Rick had put into a repetitive loop, showing off the projects they'd decided best showcased the tangible results of the artistic program. This section included sound she'd recorded at various shows she'd organized throughout the past year.

They allowed the people there to hear comments from students and their parents about how much they loved the program and would miss it if the school decided not to renew it.

Following her mother's advice, Emma paused on the final slide—a sixth-grader's Impressionist-style rendition of Liberty Creek's iconic covered bridge. It wasn't Monet, but the boy's talent was obvious, and she hoped that it would convince the board to continue funding for the program that was so dear to her heart. "So, does anyone have questions for me?"

She fielded the usual ones about whether costs would rise and was pleased to have Rick's numbers to back up her assurance that they would remain the same. Some wondered how she planned to change the offerings for the coming year, and everyone seemed more than satisfied with her responses.

Except for the board, she noticed.

There were more of those awkward looks, and a woman she'd known her entire life actually stared down at her folded hands while Emma was speaking. She had no idea what might be bothering them, but she returned to where Rick was sitting and picked up her messenger bag to go.

"Let's stick around," he murmured.

"Why?"

"Just a feeling," he replied cryptically. "Something's going on, and my hunch is we'd be smart to hang around and find out what it is."

The fact that he'd picked up on the same vibe she'd gotten was impressive, especially since he'd never attended one of these meetings before tonight. Then again, Emma thought as she sat down beside him, he'd probably been in hundreds of conferences just like it and had learned to recognize the signs of potential trouble. In his line of work, it must be a handy skill to have.

"And now," the president announced in a somber tone, "we'll address something that has unfortunately become necessary in response to our declining student enrollment and accompanying reduction in our state aid. The past few years, staffing at our elementary, middle and high schools has remained steady due to retirements and resignations. This year I'm sorry to inform you that will not be the case, and we have some very difficult decisions that must be made."

He went on to list the positions that were on the block, and Emma's heart sank when she realized that some of her colleagues were going to lose their jobs. But nothing could have prepared her for the final item on his list.

"Art teacher, elementary school."

Emma's heart stopped. Rick muttered something under his breath, and when she looked over at him, he grimaced in a silent display of sympathy.

Because she was too numb to move, they sat through the rest of the meeting while she stared down at the binder she had clasped in her arms, trying to process what she'd learned. Mercifully, it ended, and when they got outside, she turned to Rick with the one question that was foremost in her mind.

"Why didn't anyone warn me?" she demanded in a furious whisper. "They let me go up there and waste everyone's time with that stupid presentation."

"First of all," he said in a calm, reasonable tone that he must use with his daughters when they were upset, "it wasn't stupid. It was very polished and well received."

"That may be, but it was still a waste of time. Yours, mine and everyone who came tonight." He gave her a pensive look, and she blew out a frustrated breath to avoid taking out her aggravation on this generous man who'd given up so much of his scarce free time to help her.

"You're way more accustomed to this kind of thing than I am. What are you thinking?"

"You won't like it, and I could be wrong."

"Just tell me the truth."

He hesitated for a few moments, and though she was ready to burst with impatience, she recognized that he was trying to spare her feelings. "Nothing is as bad as fighting cancer, Rick. Whatever you have to say, I can handle it."

Heaving a sigh, he said, "I'm thinking that since the arts program is so popular, they might be tempted to keep it going."

It didn't take a genius to fill in the blank. "Without me."

"I don't know any of the board members, so I could be wrong," he said.

"Is that what you'd do?" she asked bluntly.

"I haven't seen the figures they're working with," he hedged. When she clucked her tongue in disdain, he relented. "It'd be one way to go. They'd save on your salary and benefits, distribute your class load to a couple of other teachers and still have the after-school option for families who want it. They could even charge a small fee to make it pay for itself."

"So the numbers would work," she commented quietly.

"I seem to recall learning recently that numbers aren't everything," Rick said, offering a compassionate smile very unlike the usual smooth, professional one she'd gotten from him before. "They have till next month's meeting to solicit comments from the community and come up with another solution. We should take advantage of that time and show them that you're too valuable for them to lose."

"But that would mean that someone else would lose their position. Lots of people who work here have families, and their kids go to school here. It would be a lot harder for them to move than it would be for me."

"That's very gracious of you," he told her, his smile warming with admiration. "But it's not fair for you to lose your job just because you're single. If you want to fight for it, I'm sure there are plenty of folks in town who'd support you. Your family, for starters, and you can count the girls and me in, too."

"Thanks. That's very sweet of you."

Feeling more than a little overwhelmed, she stared across the campus at the redbrick building where she'd attended school as a child and happily worked since graduating from college. She loved that old place, with its drafty windows and cranky heating system that kept her room at sauna temperatures all year round.

The last thing she wanted was to leave it—and her hometown—for some unknown town full of strangers. Beyond that, this was the time of year when schools were actively searching for teachers to fill open spots, and she was far from ready to apply. Funding cuts had required many of them to trim their arts offerings to free up money for academics. Some schools in the area had dropped music and art completely, relying on already overworked educators to fill in the gaps for their students.

Competition for art positions would be fierce, and she might be forced to take on a classroom part-time rather than function solely as an art teacher. Her dual certification enabled her to do that, but she hated the idea of teaching math and writing instead of nurturing budding artists in the bright, sunny classroom that had become her second home.

So, as she'd done when the doctor delivered his heart-stopping diagnosis to her, she squared her shoulders and turned to the man who'd unexpectedly become her champion. "I'm not giving up, but I won't do anything that will cause someone else to be fired in my place. Can you help me make that happen?"

"I'm not sure," he replied honestly, easing the harsh truth with a smile. "But I'll try."

Chapter Four

"Daddy."

It was barely light outside when Aubrey's whisper filtered through Rick's sleepy fog to wake him. Opening his eyes, he saw her in her floral nightgown, clutching her stuffed rabbit. Silhouetted by the glow of the night-light in the hallway, she had a concerned look on her face. "Hmm?"

"Caitlin's sick."

Instantly alert, he sat up and turned his bedside lamp on. His girls weren't prone to any kind of illness, and Caitlin loved school so much that she often disguised her discomfort so she'd be allowed to go even when she wasn't 100 percent healthy. "What's wrong?"

In answer, Aubrey tugged on his hand, and he followed her back to the dollhouse-inspired room that the girls shared. To make the move a little easier for them, he'd given them carte blanche while they'd designed their new room. Then he'd spent a solid weekend following their instructions to the letter, right down to locating the floral drapes they'd chosen in various shades of pink.

When he knelt by her bed, Caitlin's eyes drifted open and she coughed into her shoulder the way they were taught to do in school these days. "Hi, Daddy," she croaked, clearly trying to smile.

"Hey there, pumpkin." A palm on her forehead told him she was running a fever. "Not feeling too good, huh?"

"It's not time to get up yet," she pointed out in a faint voice. "I'm sure I'll feel better by then."

Rick made a show of looking over his shoulder at the display on the clock that stood on the table between the twin beds. Coming back to his brave little girl, he frowned and shook his head. "I doubt that, but let's get you some juice and something to bring down your fever. Then we'll see how you're doing later this morning. If you're not better, I'll take you to the doctor."

Already, he was rearranging his day, mentally listing things that he could handle from home and others that would have to be re-scheduled to another time. As the girls' only parent, he considered it his responsibility to be home with them when they were sick.

To his amazement, Caitlin shook her head. "No, Daddy, you need to go to the bank and help people. Mrs. Fields can take care of me."

"And I will, too," Aubrey assured him, cuddling against him for a hug. "We know what to do, Daddy."

"You go to work. I'll be fine," Caitlin added, patting his hand in a reassuring gesture that felt eerily familiar. It took him a few moments, but when he placed it, his heart nearly stopped.

Those were the last words Sarah said to him the day she died.

The situation with Caitlin was far less severe, but his gut was telling him to stay with her and make her sick day as easy as possible for her. So he forced a grin and pulled rank. "Last time I checked, I'm the dad and what I say goes. And I say I'm staying home to take care of my girl. First on the list—a thermometer and some kid's aspirin. You stay here and I'll be right back."

"Okay," she agreed meekly, rolling onto her side and pillowing her cheek on her hand.

"Don't worry about her," Aubrey told him

sweetly as she curled up at the foot of her sister's bed. "I'll take care of her, too."

"That's my girl," he approved, ticking the end of her elfin nose with his finger on his way out. By the time he got back, they were cuddled together, both curly heads resting on Caitlin's pillow. He considered separating them to keep Aubrey from getting sick, then thought better of it. They were together constantly, so chances were good that they'd be sharing this bug the way they shared everything else. If being together made them feel better, he didn't see the harm in it.

Caitlin was her usual cooperative self, taking the thermometer and grape-flavored liquid without complaint. The fever wasn't bad enough for a doctor's visit just yet, but he made a note to take it again in a couple of hours to be sure the medicine was doing its job.

Heading downstairs to the kitchen, he yawned while he canceled the coffeemaker's timer and manually set a pot brewing. Six o'clock was too early to disturb Mrs. Fields with a call, but he made some toast for the girls and lightly spread their favorite jams over top. Strawberry for Caitlin and grape for Aubrey. After delivering their very-early breakfast to their room, he grabbed a cup of much-needed caffeine and went into his office to send out some professional emails and voice mails.

When he reached Mrs. Fields around seven, she clucked her tongue in sympathy. "Now, don't you worry about a thing. I'll take care of the housework while you tend to your girls."

"I was thinking you might rather take the day off," he said, surprised by her response. She worked on salary, and he'd assumed she'd be happy to have an extra vacation day while he was home to handle her usual duties.

"Not a bit. If we work together, the day will go much better for everyone. Unless you'd rather not have me there for some reason."

"None that I can think of," he admitted, touched by her willingness to help.

While that was nice, it also underscored just how much he and his daughters were missing from their lives. For some crazy reason his memory flashed back to their impromptu dinner with Emma the other night. His eyes went to the formal dining room, which stood empty and immaculate the way it normally did. That night it had felt chaotic and fun, and he found himself wishing that it could be that way all the time.

"Then I'll see you at eight, as usual," she said briskly, bringing him back to reality.

"Is there anything I can pick up on my way through town? Something from Ellie's Bakery perhaps?"

"Blueberry muffins," he replied without thinking. Then, since he'd taken that leap, he added, "And some of those raspberry Danish she makes fresh every morning. They're the girls' favorites. And please add in whatever you'd like for yourself."

"Will do," the woman agreed with a laugh. "Anything for you?"

He wasn't a big breakfast person, usually settling for a bagel and coffee at his desk. But today he could indulge a little, and he thought through the menu at the bakery before settling on something called the Minuteman breakfast sandwich that he'd been wanting to try but never had the time for. After adding that to her list, Mrs. Fields said goodbye and hung up.

Rick's mornings were normally hectic, at best, and he wasn't sure how to spend the extra time he'd been granted. Outside the kitchen windows he saw that the sun was peeking over the trees in the backyard, and he opened the Dutch door, leaning on the top to admire the view he seldom had time to appreciate.

Large oak and maple trees that had been around for decades were coming into leaf, their branches shading sections of the yard. In others, the rental home's owners had planted gardens that were beginning to sprout flowers, and he realized that he was looking forward to seeing what varieties they turned out to be. Perfectly centered at the back of the fenced yard, the rustic wooden playset that had appealed to him online seemed to be waiting patiently for someone to come out and enjoy it.

With the nice weather seemingly here to stay, he hoped the girls would have a good time out there. Then it occurred to him that he hadn't yet tested the various pieces to make sure they were safe for them to use.

Setting his coffee on the counter, he opened the door and strolled outside. The grass was dewy, and it felt cool on his bare feet as he strolled toward the slide. A few good shakes confirmed that the structure was solid, so he moved on to the monkey bars and ladders to inspect them. Finally, he gave each of the swing chains a firm yank, satisfying himself that they were just as sturdy as the rest.

Looking up, he admired the craftsmanship that had gone into the playset. Someone had put a lot of effort into making it not only fun but also safe for the kids who'd be playing on it for years to come. He wasn't impulsive by nature, but something prompted him to sit on one of the swings, twisting the chains to spin him in a circle the way he'd done when he was a boy.

Some kind of bird squabble was going on overhead, and he glanced up to find a cardinal squawking at a blue jay who was occupied building a nest in the crook of a high branch. The blue jay didn't seem fazed by the scolding, and Rick chuckled at the haughty expression on its face.

"I must be seeing things," a woman's voice said from the other side of the quaint white picket fence. When he glanced over, Emma Calhoun was leaning on the top rail, grinning into the yard at him. "In my wildest dreams, I never imagined seeing the very buttoned-up Rick Marshall enjoying himself on a swing set."

"I'm just full of surprises," he countered, startled to hear the teasing tone in his own voice. He was a fairly serious person, and he took his responsibilities just as seriously. That he felt comfortable enough with the young art teacher to joke around was surprising, to say the least. Remembering his manners, he stood and met her near the boundary of the yard.

"What brings you over to this side of town so early?"

"It's a beautiful day," she replied as if the reason should have been obvious to him.

He'd been admiring it himself, but he didn't see the connection. "True enough, but what brings you here in particular?"

"I take a walk every morning before school, as long as the weather's decent."

During his short time in New Hampshire, Rick had learned that the locals' definition of *decent weather* was different from his, and he chuckled. "What exactly does that mean? I've been wondering ever since I got here."

"No lightning, hail or blizzard," she explained, ticking the hazards off on her fingers. Then she added a sassy grin. "For me, it also can't be too windy. I'm pretty light, and I don't want to end up in Oz."

He laughed out loud. He seemed to be doing that more and more lately. Usually, it was his girls who set him off that way, and that Emma seemed to have a knack for it baffled him. Considering all she'd been through, her light-hearted approach to life was amazing. Maybe he could take a lesson from this soft-spoken but determined woman. "Good plan."

"I think so. I've never seen you around during my strolls. Are you playing hooky today?"

Hardly, he scoffed silently. Sloughing off that way got you precisely nowhere, his father had told him from the time that he was old enough to understand the concept. Hard work and dedication had taken Philip Marshall to the top of the banking profession in his native Charleston, and his ongoing guidance was doing the same for Rick. He had no intention of taking his foot off the gas now. "Caitlin's home sick, so I'm combining work time and dad time today."

"I hope it's nothing serious. She loves school, and she must hate missing it."

"She does," he confirmed with a sigh. "She even tried to convince me to go to work, but I vetoed that idea."

"Good for you. It was brave of her to try, though. She must get that soldiering-on attitude from you."

"Actually, that's all Sarah," he said before he realized what he was doing. It wasn't like him to share personal details so easily, but now that he'd started, he couldn't deny that it felt good to open up just a bit. "Even near the end, she kept on going, doing everything she could until even the little things got to be too much for her. I still don't know how she did it."

"Because she had people counting on her," Emma answered, adding a gentle smile of understanding. "Taking care of you and the girls was important to her."

In the compassionate response, Rick caught another, more subtle, meaning. After thinking about it for a moment, he said, "I get the feeling you're talking about yourself, too."

She nodded. "My family and my students kept me going, even on the worst days. Chemo is awful, but when you have someone to focus on besides yourself, it really helps. A strong dash of faith doesn't hurt, either."

There it was again, Rick thought, the easy reference to religion that he'd picked up on from so many residents of this small town. Down-to-earth and hardworking, people here seemed to have a strong dedication to their religious beliefs, which was something he'd never developed. He and his attorney sister had been raised to be smart and successful, and they'd both done well in their respective fields. But while his parents had stressed education and hard work, he couldn't recall them ever mentioning the value of cultivating a relationship with God. Apparently, they just didn't believe that it was necessary.

Rick had shared that attitude for most of his life, until he met Sarah. Her devotion to the faith that eluded him was sweet, and while he hadn't truly understood it, he'd gone through the motions for her sake. She'd felt that it was important for Caitlin and Aubrey to attend Sunday school, and he hadn't objected. Quite honestly, he didn't care all that much one way or the other.

He enjoyed their quiet Sunday mornings, sleeping in and then making a huge stack of pancakes in whatever shapes his daughters asked him for. But now he found himself wondering if they'd like to join the local Sunday school and save their pancakes for after church.

"So," he began, feeling awkward around Emma for the first time. Her curious expression prompted him to go on, and he forced himself to sound casual. "I noticed that there are three churches in town. Which one do you and your family go to?"

"The oldest one," she replied, pointing to the modest white chapel on the far side of the town square. "My ancestors, Jeremiah Calhoun and his two brothers, built it back in the

1820s, and the family has gone to services there ever since."

"Those are the blacksmithing brothers who founded the town and put the bridge across Liberty Creek, right?" She nodded. "I got a history lesson from Sam and Brian when I stopped in at the forge over the winter," he said.

Mention of her big brothers made her beam proudly. "They're very proud to be carrying on the family business, and we're thankful that they've decided it's worth the effort to keep those old traditions going. When our cousin Jordan gets here this fall, there will be three Calhouns working around the forge, just like there were back in the beginning."

The symmetry of that appealed to Rick for some reason, and he smiled. "It sounds like things are coming full circle for Liberty Creek. It's not easy for villages like this to keep things moving forward. I've seen a few that are just a few steps short of becoming ghost towns."

"Having our own school is an important part of our future," she commented in a quiet but determined voice. "They've talked about merging with Fairfield, another small district near here, but so far we've been able to avoid that. Others haven't been so lucky, and while I'm sure that it makes sense financially, it's tough on the people who lose that part of their community."

"I can only imagine."

Behind him, he heard an upper window creak open and glanced back to find Aubrey framed in the girls' window. "Daddy?"

"What is it, sweetie?"

"Caitlin just threw up. She was trying to get to the bathroom."

It didn't take a genius to fill in that blank, and Rick turned back to the delightful visitor who'd brought an unexpected ray of sunshine into his morning. "That's my cue. Thanks for stopping to chat."

"Go on," she replied, waving him off. "Give Caitlin a hug from me and tell her that I hope she's feeling better soon."

"Will do."

As Emma continued her walk, Rick hurried back inside to take care of his sick little girl. It wasn't his favorite type of dad duty, but when his daughters needed him, he knew that his place was with them. Sarah, through her quiet courage and unending love for them all, had taught him that.

And now that she was gone, he was grateful for the wisdom she'd left behind.

* * *

Friday morning Emma turned the corner near the Marshalls' rental house and got the surprise of her week.

There, next to the wrought iron gate that led to the front walkway, stood Rick. Holding a paper plate of what looked to be her Gran's famous orange-cranberry muffins and a coffee mug that read "World's Awesomest Dad," he grinned as if this was something he did every day. "Morning. Mind if I walk along with you?"

She couldn't have been more shocked if he'd starting turning cartwheels in the middle of the deserted street, but one thing she'd learned during her career of working with kids: no matter what happens, just roll with it.

"This is a free country," she teased as he fell in step beside her. "You can walk wherever and whenever you want."

He looked taken aback by her response, so she added a bright smile to make sure he knew she was teasing him. She reminded herself that he was a solemn person by nature, and she didn't want to do anything that might make him feel self-conscious around her. Why that mattered, she wasn't completely sure, but her instincts had never led her astray before, and she wasn't about to start ignoring them now.

"Thanks," he said in a relieved voice. "Some people would rather have their solitude, so I wasn't sure you'd be open to company so early in the day."

She laughed at the thought. "Oh, I've been up for hours. I like to paint when it's quiet."

"I like to sleep when it's quiet," he confided, clearly trying to swallow a yawn. "When you've got two busy girls, you have to grab a few winks whenever you can."

"Sounds smart to me. How is Caitlin feeling?"

"Better, but now Aubrey has that bug, and Cait wanted to stay home to take care of her. So I'm playing hooky, too. I figured since it's Friday, there was no harm in us making a long weekend for ourselves."

"Is Mrs. Fields not available?"

"No, she's there. That's not the same as being there myself, though."

His voice had drifted in a pensive direction, and she wondered what he was thinking. Rick had struck her as a nose-to-the-grindstone kind of guy, and everything from his sleek laptop to his mirror-polish shoes marked him as the stereotypical ambitious banker. It seemed odd that he'd relax those rules for a simple child-hood illness. Her intuition told her that there was more to it than fatherly concern, but she recognized that his reasons were absolutely none of her business.

Because she didn't know how else to react, she simply said, "That's true."

They fell silent, and she suddenly felt awk-ward strolling through town with the new-comer who'd caused such a stir since arriving in Liberty Creek during the winter. He'd ar-ranged funding for Liberty Creek Forge when her brother was struggling to reopen their fam-ily's vintage blacksmith shop and make it prof-itable. She'd also heard that Rick had signed off on some refinancing arrangements to keep local families from losing their homes due to the poor economy. Then there were folks who insisted he was a heartless Scrooge who valued dollar signs more than human beings.

Chances were, like most people, he was a blend of many qualities, good and bad. But so far, she'd seen a lot more of the former, and she was inclined to give him the benefit of the doubt. Reaching over, she grabbed a muffin from the paper plate and took an enormous bite. Humming in appreciation, she swallowed it and sighed. "I've been eating these my entire life, and I still don't know how she does it."

"Lard," Rick answered, chuckling as he took a bite of his own. "That's all she'd tell me, though, and she winked when she said it."

"That means there's a lot of it in the batter," Emma explained with a laugh. "Gran doesn't worry much about cholesterol. She firmly believes that God has already mapped out your lifetime for you, and however long it is, you should enjoy everything to the hilt."

In between bites, he made a noise that she took as agreement. Then, to her surprise, he quietly said, "Sarah was like that, too. I'm more cautious, I guess. The day she decided to stop her chemo was the worst day of my life."

Halting in midstride, Emma stared up at him in disbelief. "She did what?"

He fixed Emma with a helpless look. "There was nothing I could do. I argued, pleaded, yelled, threatened. In the end, it was her decision. So I took her home from the hospital and brought in the best full-time nurse I could find. Three months later Sarah was gone."

The agony lining his face told Emma that there was more to the story, and she debated whether to push him any further. But he'd opened up to her so much already, she thought it might help him to get it all out. "That must have been incredibly hard on all of you."

"The girls were younger, and they knew their mommy was sick," he replied in a voice barely above a whispcr. "I was at a major meeting one afternoon, and the nurse called to tell me Sarah had taken a bad turn. I broke every speed limit to get home in time." After a long breath to steady his shaking voice, he finished. "I didn't make it."

"Oh, Rick." Overcome by the emotions radiating from this very pragmatic man, she rested a hand on his arm, hoping to comfort him a bit. "How awful for you."

"I can never go back and change that," he said, his voice now flat with resignation. Straightening his shoulders, he seemed to almost shake off the past in a gesture Emma knew only too well. "So now, when one of the girls is sick, I stay home. I know the flu isn't leukemia, but it makes me feel better knowing that I'm there if they need me."

"They always need you," Emma reminded him, rubbing his arm in sympathy. "Even grown-up girls need their daddies. I can tell you that from personal experience."

Rick's stony features softened into a genuine smile totally unlike the practiced one she'd seen so often from him. "I met your father over at the forge. He was helping Sam and Brian frame in that new display area Lindsay wants to use for their ironworking demonstrations. Steve seems like a good guy."

"The best. He and my mother, Melinda, were high school sweethearts, and they taught us all about how precious a strong family is. I never would've gotten through my treatments without their support, and they've been great during all this upheaval at school over my job. I don't know where I'd be without them."

"Family's nice," he agreed as they resumed their circuit of the village. "Mine is scattered around, but we get together at my aunt and uncle's place on Martha's Vineyard every summer. It's a lot of fun."

"I love it there. Between the beautiful scenery and all those colorful people, I could paint every single day and never run out of things to capture."

"I'm not the creative type," he told her again, adding a chuckle. "Mostly I enjoy being on the beach, sailing out on the ocean and fresh lobster."

"I did a painting of a sailboat regatta they held one time when I was there. I'll show it to you sometime and if you like it, it's yours.

You can hang it on that big, blank wall opposite the landscape you already bought. It'll help brighten up your office."

He slanted her a boyish grin that she wouldn't have believed he was capable of if she hadn't seen it with her own eyes. "If it's as good as I think it is, I wouldn't waste it on the bank. It'll go in the living room."

Stunned, she blinked a couple of times, trying to regain her composure. "Well, I guess you can hang it wherever you want."

"I'll do that. Thanks."

"You're welcome."

"Speaking of the bank, though," he continued as they turned onto Chestnut Street, "I had an idea yesterday that I wanted to run past you."

She wasn't exactly a financial wiz, so no one ever asked her opinion on anything even remotely related to money. His request caught Emma by surprise, but she did her best to appear as though she was fine with it. "Okay. Shoot."

"The situation at the school is more complicated than just shifting funds from one place to another to cover the positions that are in jeopardy. I was hoping you and the others involved might have some suggestions on where we can look for solutions."

Emma's jaw dropped, and she carefully closed it before asking, "You want our input?" When he nodded, she frowned in confusion. "But we're teachers. You're the numbers guy."

"True, but I don't know how things work there day-to-day. It may be that you'll be able to highlight opportunities I wouldn't even think of because I'm not an employee."

She recognized the professional-speak he'd slipped into from their first meeting at the bank, and while she followed his general meaning, she was concerned that his usual mode of presentation would be sorely lacking for regular folks. "I think it's a good idea, but I have a couple of suggestions for you."

"Okay. Shoot."

He added a grin that told her he'd intentionally echoed her earlier comment, and she couldn't help smiling. For all his boardroom appearance, apparently Rick Marshall still had a playful side. She wondered what it would take to get him to loosen up and let it out more often. Not that she was the one to be doing that, of course. It was just a matter of curiosity for her.

"First," she ticked her forefinger, "you need

to keep it simple. I think it's easy for you to get into the details and forget that you're talking about people's lives, not just numbers on a spreadsheet. They're scared about losing their jobs and their incomes, so you'll have to be sensitive about that."

"Got it. What else?"

"Lots of people view going to consult with a banker as a step above a root canal. If we do the meeting at the bank, they'll be half terrified before they even get there. I think we should have it at my house some evening and serve plenty of snacks. Everything goes down better with one of Gran's yummy desserts."

He thought it over then said, "Excellent suggestions. Now I have one for you."

"What's that?"

Stopping in the middle of the sidewalk, he smiled down at her. "Have a good day."

"What?"

Their running conversation had kept her so preoccupied, she hadn't noticed that they'd finished their tour of the town and had ended up in front of her house. Feeling more than a little foolish, she laughed. "I totally lost track of where we were."

Cocking his head in an inquisitive pose, he asked, "Is that a good thing?"

She considered that for a moment, then smiled. "Yes, it is."

"Good, because I enjoyed it, too. I can't remember the last time one of my mornings started out so nicely. Thank you, Emma."

"You're welcome."

Watching him stroll away, she found herself wondering what on earth had just happened. Apparently, the well-starched, tightly wound banker had a softer side that he'd chosen to share with her.

Why her, she had no clue. But she felt honored that he trusted her enough to do it.

Chapter Five

Sunday morning.

Usually, this was the one day of the week when Rick allowed himself to stay in bed for a while, drifting in and out of a light doze until his daughters bounded across the hallway and woke him up. On this particular Sunday, though, he had other ideas. Emma's mention of a Sunday school at the Liberty Chapel had caught his interest, and ever since then he'd been toying with the idea of attending a service there, just to see how it went.

If the girls liked it, he didn't mind continuing to go. If not, he wouldn't miss it, either. He had a suspicion that being ambivalent about religion wasn't appropriate for a dad, but he wasn't one to pretend that he valued something simply because it made him look good.

He also wouldn't keep them from going if they got something out of it. Just because he didn't see the point didn't mean they had to miss out on what it might have to offer them.

In his imagination, he heard Sarah's unmistakable laughter. At least he assumed that it was his imagination. There were times when he could almost feel her presence close by, and more than once he'd wondered if that feeling was more than wishful thinking. Then the moment would pass, and he'd feel like an idiot for allowing himself to believe something so impossible, no matter how brief his lapse in common sense might have been. She'd been part of his life for so long, it was understandable that her memory would continue to influence him in some way.

At least that was what he told himself.

He flung those fanciful thoughts aside with the covers and got himself ready for a new venture that would probably prove to be a waste of time. At least he knew the Calhouns, he reasoned as he combed out his wet hair. As generous as Emma and her family had been to them so far, he had no doubt that they'd welcome his girls and him into their church with open arms.

The door across the hall stood partially closed, and he knocked before opening it the rest of the way. Caitlin stirred and rolled over to yawn at him. "Morning, Daddy."

"Morning. How're you doing?"

"Fine. What's up?"

"How'd you like to come to church with me?"

At the sound of his voice, Aubrey stretched out to her full length before curling up like a sleepy kitten. Blinking her eyes open, she stared over at him in confusion. "What church?"

"Emma and her family go to the Liberty Chapel near the square," he explained. "She invited us to come by sometime, and I was thinking today might be good."

"I like Emma," Aubrey informed him with a yawn. "She's so pretty and nice."

She'd summed up his own impression of the soft-spoken artist, and he grinned. "Yeah, she is. So, would you ladies like to come with me?"

Caitlin sat up and gave him a curious once-over. "We haven't gone to church since Mommy went to heaven."

"I know," he said, swallowing hard around the lump that had suddenly formed in his throat. "Maybe it's time for us to try it again."

"Because Emma will be there?"

Caitlin's innocent question caught him by

surprise, and it dawned on Rick that, in a way, that was the reason for his change of heart. "She invited us, so I guess that's as good a reason as any."

"We wouldn't want to disappoint Emma," his older girl agreed, swinging out of bed before heading to her closet. "Come on, Aubrey. I'll help you pick out a dress and then Daddy can do your hair."

"Okay."

Aubrey bounced to her feet, obviously excited by the prospect of breaking their usual mellow Sunday routine. Their enthusiasm was infectious, and Rick found himself humming while he pulled bowls and their favorite cereals from the cupboard. His usual coffee and a bagel didn't appeal to him much lately, so he added a third setting for himself. He was halfway through a bowl of vitamin-fortified sugar when the girls joined him. They didn't say anything, but their astonished looks clearly said that he'd surprised them with his change in routine.

They chatted while they ate, and he downed a bracing jolt of caffeine before tackling the brushing and French-braiding of two heads of long blond hair. When he was done, he sat back and smiled. "Y'know, I think I have the most beautiful daughters on the planet."

Caitlin laughed. "You always say that."

"Then you say how much we look like Mommy," Aubrey chimed in, glancing over her shoulder at a picture of them with Sarah that hung on the wall. She had the expression of someone looking at a photo of a stranger, and his heart twisted with regret.

He'd done his best to keep their mother alive for them, but it killed him that his four-year-old had no personal memories of her. Every time he looked at one of his daughters, he saw the woman who'd given them every bit of love and energy she had, right until the end of her life. He only wished he could give them half as much as Sarah had. He tried, but he knew they were missing out on so much, not having a mother. They needed a woman to talk with, confide their secrets to, share their triumphs and heartaches.

He loved them endlessly, but at the end of the day, he was still a guy. It just wasn't the same.

Pushing those pointless thoughts aside, he glanced at the clock and stood. "We don't want to be late for our first day of church. Let's all clean up and get ready to go."

They followed his lead without complaint, which told him how eager they were to try something new. They were such troupers, he mused proudly while they brushed their teeth and found their shoes. So much had changed for them in the past two years, sometimes he wondered if he was asking too much of them. Days like these let him know that for all the challenges they'd faced, his sweet, resilient girls were doing fine.

The church was only a few blocks away, so they decided to walk. They weren't the only ones, he noticed, and several families greeted them on their way up the street. The quaint white chapel was nestled beneath some of the largest, most brilliant red maples he'd ever seen. Everything in Liberty Creek dated back to the early 1820s, and it was easy to picture long-ago families walking in from their homes to attend services the same way their modern counterparts were doing now.

Similar to many of the other structures in town, the little church was a bit faded, its tall windows showing some wear and tear around the colorful windows. He wondered if Jordan Calhoun's talent for stained glass would be tapped for some repairs once he got to town. The roof looked new to Rick, but some shutters that had blown off during the harsh winter were still missing, and the concrete steps could use some attention from an expert. The building reminded him of the residents of this picturesque New England town: sturdy and weathered by time.

That thought had just passed through his mind when he heard a familiar laugh and caught sight of someone who definitely didn't fit that description. Emma Calhoun was strolling in with Lindsay and Brian, who held an adorable baby wearing a cotton candy–pink dress. A red pickup came down Main Street, slowing to come alongside the little group. Sam and his wife, Holly, were in the cab, their son Chase sitting between them. The two groups stopped in the middle of Main Street to chat, and Rick couldn't help grinning. Anywhere else he'd lived, that kind of dawdling would have caused an instant traffic jam and some serious temper tantrums. Here, it was a daily occurrence, and no one seemed to think anything of it.

It was hard for him to believe that he'd gradually become accustomed to the slower pace of life here in rural New Hampshire. Not only that, he realized suddenly, he actually liked it. People took the time to enjoy their days, connecting with family and friends whenever the opportunity presented itself. Their approach to life was a major shift from the bustling, ambitious people he'd known before, and he admired them for keeping their old-fashioned values in a world that often seemed determined to destroy them.

He'd only planned on staying in Liberty Creek long enough to get the bank's new branch solidly on its feet and then move on to the next assignment that his boss had in mind for him. But lately he'd begun pondering whether this might be a nice place to raise his girls, away from the chaos that plagued so many of the cities he'd visited, no matter where they were. Here, they could walk up the street to the park without him worrying about the traffic, because there just wasn't that much. Quiet and unassuming, it was the kind of home that he'd never considered before, but he had to admit that it was growing on him.

Especially the people, he thought as Emma flashed them a bright smile and hurried up the sidewalk to meet them.

"Good morning!" she sang, leaning in to wrap the girls in a warm hug before straightening to gaze up at Rick. "How nice to see you all here."

She didn't say anything beyond that, but her sparkling blue eyes made it plain that she was delighted to see them. He couldn't recall the last time anyone had made him feel as special as Emma did. Women usually looked him over with interest, noticed his wedding band, then pulled away. Emma's approach to him was proof that she didn't consider him anything other than a friend, which was a refreshing change.

"You picked the perfect day to come," she went on, leading them toward the double front doors. "Holly and Lindsay are doing Sunday school, and I hear they have something really fun planned for the kids."

Rick had assumed that his daughters would sit with him, and he was just about to tell her that when Caitlin exclaimed, "That would be awesome!"

Aubrey, who was more reserved by nature, boldly asked, "Will Chase be there?"

"Absolutely," Emma assured her. "He's in charge of the snacks."

"Last time we saw him at the bakery, he let me look at one of his animal books," Aubrey went on in a rare show of bravery. "Do you think he brought one of them today?"

"If he didn't, there are some in the church

library. I'd imagine he'll help you pick one out if you want."

"I like Chase," Aubrey announced, adding a dimpled smile. "I don't have a big brother, but he'd be a nice one."

Rick was stunned by her comment, but he managed to hide his shock when his shy girl glanced up at him. "Can I go to Sunday school with Caitlin, Daddy? Please?"

"Of course you can, sweetness. I think it's a great idea."

"You'll make some new friends, Froggy," Caitlin said, squeezing her around the shoulders in a big-sister gesture. "Then when you start preschool in the fall, you'll already know some of the other kids. That will make it easier."

Preschool. Rick barely stifled a sigh as Emma led them to a pew in the front already half filled with Calhouns. His girls were growing up so fast, sometimes he lost track of how quickly the time was slipping by.

"It goes by fast, doesn't it?" Emma asked quietly.

He chuckled. "Was it that obvious?"

"The look on your face just now said it all. Kids have a way of growing up when we're not looking. Sometimes my students come back to visit after they've gone onto the middle and high schools, and I can't believe they're the same people. The petite teacher held up a hand far over her head and laughed. "I need a step-ladder to look some of them in the eyes."

"They really come back to see you?" he asked, sliding over to make room for the girls beside him.

"Some of them do. Others write or email, or text me photos of their latest projects. It's rewarding to know that I had an impact on them when they were younger, and that as they're growing up, they haven't forgotten about me."

Rick couldn't imagine anyone forgetting Emma Calhoun after talking to her for five minutes, much less after spending years in her bright, creative classroom or after-school program. She was the kind of person who made the world a better place merely by being in it. Watching her with his own daughters had given him a close-up view of how she nurtured children's talents, encouraging them to try new things, making them laugh.

Come to think of it, he mused as he opened a hymnal, she'd done the same for him. How she'd managed that, he wasn't quite sure, but he definitely felt more a part of the community since he'd volunteered to help her. Apparently, she had a knack for drawing people out, no matter how young or old they were. Being more of a pragmatic person, it was a skill that he didn't share, and he wasn't too proud to admit that he was a little envious of her.

In the row in front of him, the head of this raucous family turned and offered a beefy hand. "Not sure you remember, but I'm Emma's dad, Steve Calhoun."

"Hard to forget seeing you dangling from the rafters at the forge, installing that exhaust fan," Rick replied as they shook. "It's nice to see you back on solid ground."

"Yeah, that was a project," he commented with a chortle. "Sometimes I think Sam and Brian come up with those jobs just to see if their old man can still hack the tough stuff."

"Aw, come on," Brian objected. "You lost the toss for going up there, and you know it."

The twinkle in Steve's eyes confirmed his son's version of the story, and he laughed. "So, how're things at Patriots Bank these days?"

"Busy," Rick answered proudly. "More customers come in every week, and I've written up several mortgages for buyers who are moving into the area. That's not only good for business, it also tells us that people want to come here to raise their kids."

"Which means they'll be sticking around a while," Emma's oldest brother, Sam, added with a nod. "That's good for everyone, especially contractors like me."

"And teachers," Emma chimed in enthusiastically. "Which is why the school needs to find a way to keep the experienced ones we already have."

"Amen to that," someone behind them said. Emma turned, and the woman went on, "The Fire Department Ladies' Auxiliary is putting a petition together to circulate at our picnic next weekend. We're trading a free dessert for a signature from anyone over eighteen, so we'll have plenty of support for you and the others."

"What a fabulous idea, Gladys," Emma approved, reaching over to clasp the woman's gnarled hand warmly. "Thank you so much."

"I worked in the school office for thirty-seven years," the woman reminded her, faded eyes crinkling in a nostalgic smile. "I know how important good, caring teachers are to the kids. The future for them will be tough, and they're going to need all the help they can get to prepare them for what's ahead."

They chatted pleasantly about her grandchildren and goings-on around town, the same way other people around them were doing. It occurred to Rick that the Sunday service was about more than the sermon. It was a time for busy people to get together and trade news, offer encouragement or just be together. The churches that he'd attended with Sarah had been much bigger, and they hadn't known anyone, so other than polite exchanges with equally polite strangers, they'd mostly talked to each other. This was a different experience entirely, and he found himself warming up to the idea of making this a weekly outing for his family.

The organist started playing some warm-up chords, and the milling congregation made their way to various seats around the small chapel. It looked to him as if the families had their own sections, and he was glad to be included among the Calhoun clan. Again, he got the feeling of belonging, even though he'd never been in this church before.

The choir filed into their places behind the pastor's lectern, and as the sunlight streamed in, he noticed the details in the beautiful stained glass window behind the simple altar. It was fairly large, and the arched shape depicted the covered bridge the long-ago Calhoun brothers had built to make access across the creek easier. Beside it was their blacksmith shop and the winding lane that had originally led into the main part of town.

Everything looked the same now, he realized, except that the road was pavement instead of dirt. Having moved several times during his own life, he couldn't imagine what it must be like to live in a place that hadn't changed appreciably since it had been founded so many generations before. The residents of this small town were a sturdy, self-reliant lot, proud of their past and doing everything they could to keep the craziness of modern existence at bay.

Ordinarily, he was all for progress, believing that if you're not advancing, you're retreating. But here in Liberty Creek, newer wasn't necessarily better. It was interesting that here, in a small white chapel in the middle of the New Hampshire woods, he'd discovered a different way of looking at the world. Glancing over at his daughters, he saw their blond heads together over the pictures in a children's book of Bible stories while their new white shoes swung in rhythm. And for the first time since moving here, he saw what he'd been hoping to see.

They were happy.

Not long ago he'd been wondering if they'd

ever recover from losing their mother at such tender ages. His own mourning had been daunting enough for him to go through, but seeing them so grief stricken had broken his heart on a daily basis for months. Eventually, he got used to their unexpected bouts of sadness, the tears that had often seemed to spring up out of nowhere. Settling into their new home had been challenging, but now—finally—Caitlin and Aubrey were content.

That did more to lift his own spirits than anything else possibly could, and he glanced up toward the heaven where he'd told them their mother now lived. Watching over them, making sure they were doing well. And for the first time since her death, thinking of Sarah made him feel better instead of worse. He felt a soft touch on his shoulder and looked over, thinking it was one of the girls trying to get his attention.

But there was nothing there.

He was a practical man, so it was hard for him to believe that somehow his late wife had reached out to him, comforting him with a touch. But hard as he tried, he couldn't come up with another explanation.

So he put the odd occurrence out of his mind and focused on the words to "Old Rugged Cross."

* * *

When it was time for the girls to go downstairs for Sunday school, Emma waved goodbye and told them to have fun. It was so cute, watching the kids follow Holly and Lindsay from the chapel in a giggling, whispering line. Caitlin and Aubrey glanced back, waving at their father as if to reassure him that they'd be fine without him. For his part, Rick watched them protectively, his eyes somber even though he grinned back at them. When they were no longer in sight, he turned his attention back to the front with an audible sigh.

"They'll be fine," Emma reassured him, adding a smile. "They're also gonna have a great time with Chase and the other kids."

He grimaced but gave a single nod, returning her smile with a half-hearted one of his own. It must be hard, she thought, being a single father when he'd planned on sharing their childhood with Sarah. Instead, he was clearly still grieving her loss, not only for himself but his girls, too.

Impulsively, Emma reached out and lightly squeezed his hand in what she hoped would come across as a comforting gesture. To her surprise, his fingers grasped hers for a brief moment before letting go. His gaze was fixed on Pastor Welch, so Emma wasn't sure what that grip was all about. Maybe she'd imagined it.

She put the incident aside and shifted her focus to the sermon.

"Family comes in many forms," the preacher told them, smiling as his gaze swept through the standing-room-only church. "There are those we're born to, and those we choose for ourselves later on." Pausing, he glanced over at his wife, who beamed back at him. Facing forward again, he went on, "The ones we select often become just as precious to us as those we were raised by, because we have the option of leaving them if we want to. When we decide to stay instead and work things through, the bond between us gets stronger. Not by chance, but by choice."

Rick shifted in his seat, and Emma peeked over to find him nodding slightly. Apparently, something in those words resonated with him, and she was dying to know what it was. She'd never ask him about it, of course, but her curiosity was humming all the same. As someone who'd been raised with a strong faith in God and His great works, she had a difficult time understanding Rick's self-proclaimed ambivalence about religion. If he'd been touched by the simple, direct sermon this morning, she wondered if there was a possibility that he might find his way toward embracing the faith that meant so much to her.

Her last boyfriend had been on the fence about God, and it had always been a bone of contention for them as a couple. Her cancer diagnosis hadn't helped the situation any, and when he'd confessed to her that he couldn't deal with it, his revelation hadn't surprised her. Handsome and charming, he was a fun guy to be around, but she'd learned that there wasn't much to him beyond that. In a way, his leaving had been a blessing in disguise for her. They were headed precisely nowhere, and he'd saved her the trouble of coming up with a good reason to break things off.

Rick would never abandon someone who needed him.

Where on earth had that come from? Emma wondered, feeling self-conscious about even thinking something like that. She didn't know him all that well, but what she had learned made her confident in her assessment, even though it seemed premature for her to be making it. His devotion to his daughters was obvious, and while it pained her to see him still grieving for his late wife, she admired him for remaining true to Sarah's memory. The gold ring that glinted on his left hand was a tribute to the life that had ended far too soon, and Emma thought it was the most romantic thing she'd ever heard of. Sad, but sweet. Like the man sitting beside her.

Staring down at her from above, she realized with a jolt as those deep blue eyes bore into hers with a curious glint. Cocking his head, he gave her a questioning look, and she felt herself blushing as she belatedly stood up and joined the others in midchorus of "How Great Thou Art." The last time she'd fazed out in church, she was about ten, so it was more than a little embarrassing to be caught doing it now. From the corner of her eye, she caught her mother eyeing her strangely, and she smiled back to reassure her that there was nothing wrong.

When they all sat back down, Pastor Welch began the announcements with the usual birthdays, anniversaries and upcoming events happening around town. Then he put his hands in the pockets of his gray trousers and let out a heavy, theatrical sigh. "As many of you know, our little church is in need of some love these days. While God's grace fills this room, He's left it up to us to keep the walls of His house in good condition. There's a clipboard going around now, and I hope you'll all take a close look at it to see which jobs you'd be qualified to help us with. We need everything from construction and painting to refreshments and willing hands for cleanup, so there are spots for everyone to fill, whatever your abilities might be."

While he went on with other news, the sheets went through the congregation, row by row. When Rick flipped through to write his name on the Painting page, Emma raised her eyebrow in disbelief. "Seriously?"

"I worked my way through college painting houses," he shot back with a grin.

"So you're more than just a nice suit and a fancy briefcase?"

He took the teasing with a good-natured grin. "I guess that'd depend on who you ask."

A laugh burst free before she could stop it, which earned her some disapproving looks from the people seated nearby. Mouthing, "Sorry," she took the clipboard from him and passed it along.

"Nothing there for you?" he asked quietly.

"The high school art teacher and I are working on the mural in the back of the sanctuary," she explained, nodding toward the fading artwork on the rear wall. "It's the original, and it really needs to be properly cleaned and re-touched so it will last another two hundred years."

"You know how to do something like that?"

His question irked her for some reason, and she straightened to her full height beside him. "Yes, I do. I went to college, too, you know."

"I do know," he assured her in an apologetic tone. "And I'm impressed that your talents include restoring art as well as creating it."

Well, that was different, she conceded, feeling a bit foolish for getting her back up over nothing. People misjudged her often enough, she should be used to it by now. It could be vexing, being Sam and Brian's little sister, judged by people who'd known her since the day she was born. Sometimes she pondered what it would be like to move away and start over in a place where no one knew her or her family and had no preconceived notions about her and what she was capable of.

Rick had done that, she reasoned, making his own way, furthering his career while he raised his daughters. It had turned out well for him, and she couldn't help speculating if she might be able to do the same for herself.

She'd never seriously considered making a

life anywhere other than Liberty Creek. Familiar and comfortable, this sleepy, tight-knit community was all she'd ever known. While she didn't picture herself in the bedlam of New York City or Boston, there were other, smaller cities with vibrant artistic communities that appealed to her. During her college years, she'd visited New Haven, Connecticut, and Providence, Rhode Island, with her friends. She'd loved spending time in the galleries and museums, envisioning her own work hanging on their walls. In her hometown, she'd always be sweet little Emma Calhoun, the elementary school art teacher. Until her job had been put on the chopping block, she'd always assumed that she'd spend her entire career here.

But what if Rick's efforts failed and she was forced to start over again somewhere else? Now that she'd stared that monster in the face, the concept didn't seem quite as scary to her as it had at first. A devoted optimist, she was a firm believer that when God closed a door, He opened a window. Maybe the unpredictable situation that she'd been viewing as a problem was actually an opportunity for her to decide what she really wanted.

If fighting cancer had taught her anything, it was that life didn't have to remain the way it was to be fulfilling. The future might be different from the past, but that didn't necessarily make it bad.

Accepting that just might make the eventual outcome of the school board's deliberations easier for her to accept. Whatever it was, she knew that she'd find a way to be all right. Because she was a Calhoun, and for generations Calhouns had taken their blows and soldiered on. That undefeatable spirit was a family legacy that she had every intention of honoring.

Just as she made her silent vow, she realized that the service was over. She was grateful that her parents no longer asked her questions about what she'd learned in church that morning, the way they had when she was younger. Today she'd have no choice other than to 'fess up about her wandering mind, and that would have been embarrassing, to say the least. Caitlin and Aubrey hurried through the milling crowd, crashing into Rick and bookending him in a jubilant double hug.

"I love Sunday school, Daddy!" shy Aubrey exclaimed, brilliant blue eyes shining with joy. "I made two new friends, and their names are Frannie and Gracie. They're going to the playground in the square now. Can we go, too?"

"It's time for lunch, sweetness."

"Pleeease," she begged, folding her hands in an imploring gesture that would melt the heart of an ice statue. "Just for a little while?"

Rick glanced at Caitlin, and she shrugged. "It's fine with me. My friend Hannah will be there with her little brother, so I can hang out with her."

"Well, I guess we're going to the playground, then," he conceded, chuckling as his girls raced for the door. Turning to Emma, he asked, "Would you like to go, too?"

The casual invitation was the last thing she would have expected, and at first she wasn't sure how to respond. It wasn't like they were a couple, and he was obliged to include her in his plans. Then her brain kicked into gear, and she said, "Oh, that's family time. I'd hate to be a third wheel."

"Technically, you'd be the fourth wheel," he corrected her, adding a mischievous grin she'd never seen on him before. "And if you want to come, we'd love to have you. The girls, I mean," he amended quickly.

Combined with the earlier grasping of her hand, his slip made her curious about what he might be thinking, and she debated asking him about it. After a quick mental tug-of-war, she decided that it couldn't hurt to find out what was going on behind those intelligent eyes. While they followed after the girls at a more sedate pace, she summoned an easygoing tone. "What about you?"

"What about me?"

Glaring over at him, she shook her head. "Are you honestly that clueless, or are you just messing with me?"

He hesitated, then laughed out loud. "Okay, you got me. It's nice to have another grown-up to talk to, and you're great company."

Emma didn't hear that very often, and she couldn't quite believe it now. "Really? But I'm so quiet."

"And funny and sweet," he informed her in that mellow, almost-Southern accent of his. As they crossed the street and joined the people gathering around the playground, he gave her another boyish grin. "I have to say, I've never met anyone quite like you, Emma. You're one of a kind."

She laughed. "Does that work on the other women you've known?"

Suddenly, the humor left his expression, and he met her gaze with a direct, very intense, one of his own. A mixture of fondness and sorrow, it cast a shadow over what had started out as a lighthearted exchange between friends. "Only one."

Feeling horrible for dredging up sad memories for him, Emma waited a beat before responding. "Sarah?" When he nodded, she took a deep breath to steady her voice. "I'm honored. May I ask you something?"

A little of the darkness lifted, and he shrugged much the way Caitlin had earlier. "Sure."

"Do you think you'll ever be able to think of her and smile?"

He took a moment to consider that and nodded. "Someday. People tell me the pain eases, but I didn't believe that. Until recently, anyway."

"What changed recently?"

The corner of his mouth quirked in a half grin, and something she couldn't describe glittered in his eyes. Then in a flash it was gone, and he glanced over to where his daughters were running across the wooden suspension bridge, playing follow-the-leader with their friends. Coming back to Emma, he said, "We left Richmond and moved to Liberty Creek. A lot of things have changed since then."

Emma got the distinct impression that there was more to it than that, but when he didn't offer any more of an explanation, she decided that it was best to leave things as they were. She liked Rick, and under different circumstances she might have been open to having a romantic relationship with him.

But he had a demanding career and two wonderful daughters to raise, and Emma's future was far from certain, both personally and professionally. If she ended up losing her job—or her battle with leukemia—she didn't want to drag anyone else down with her. The path forward for her was murky at best, and while she could accept that for herself because she didn't have a choice, she'd never dream of forcing it on anyone else.

So at least for now, she was better off keeping the very appealing single father at a distance. Teaching her students, wherever they might be, sharing her love of art and encouraging them to explore their own creativity because the world could never have enough bright, beautiful things.

When she was first diagnosed, that approach to life had felt right to her. But now, for some reason, it had a hollow ring to it. She wasn't sure what had changed in the meantime, but the conclusion that had once left her feeling satisfied was now making her feel the opposite.

Why, she couldn't say. But she wasn't one to ignore her emotions, and on this sunny Sunday, she just felt sad.

Chapter Six

Emma's small living room was filled to near-bursting.

She'd pushed the artwork back to make room for some chairs and a low table to hold snacks, expecting no more than a few people. Somehow, the low-key meeting she'd arranged for Rick and the teachers whose jobs were in jeopardy had morphed into over a dozen people, each of whom had brought along their own ideas of what to do. The minimal treats she'd picked up from the bakery earlier were long gone, and she slipped into the kitchen to place a culinary SOS.

"Gran, I need your help," she began, smiling at Ellie Calhoun's infectious laughter on the other end of the phone.

"Anything for you, baby doll. What can I

do?" Emma wasn't sure what she needed, so she relayed the number of guests that she was unexpectedly entertaining and the fact that her own fridge held nothing beyond lunchmeat and some condiments so old that their expiration dates were illegible. "I've been so busy, I haven't had a chance to grocery shop."

"I know, but you really need to make time for it," her grandmother chided gently. "You're under a lot of stress, and you need to make sure you eat well. We don't want you getting sick."

Emma had been eating some of her dinners with the Marshalls, but for some reason she was hesitant to mention that to anyone. Then again, it wouldn't take long for Rick's neighbors to become aware of her frequent visits there, so before too much longer, everyone would assume—

What? she wondered. That they were seeing each other? It wasn't true, of course, but she knew that denying the rumor would only add to the buzz. The best approach would be to ignore it all and live her life the same way she had before she ever met him. She'd never cared much about what folks thought of her, after all. If fighting cancer had taught her anything, she'd learned what was truly important to her and what just didn't matter all that much.

Let the gossips spread around whatever they wanted, she thought as she went back into her crowded living room. She knew the truth about her relationship with Rick, and that was all that mattered to her.

"I don't know about this idea of yours, Emma," Dina Thompson commented with a sour look. "Working with Rick Marshall? My neighbors went to him for a personal loan a couple of weeks back, and after making them jump through all kinds of hoops, he ended up turning them down. They told me he's a pretty cold fish."

"I've heard the same thing," another woman chimed in, scowling in obvious disapproval. "All numbers, no heart."

Emma instantly jumped to his defense. "I'm sure there were good, logical reasons for them not getting the loans they requested. Rick has a responsibility to the bank to make sure their money is used well. Besides, he's coming to this meeting on his own time, to help us devise a strategy for saving our jobs." Winging a look around the group of teachers seated on her mismatched pieces of hand-me-down furniture, she summoned her mother's infamous don't-mess-with-me look. "Maybe you should wait to hear what he has to say and form your own opinions instead of taking idle gossip for the truth."

"That's easy for you to say," Dina huffed, sitting back and crossing her arms. "You don't have a family to worry about."

Emma tried very hard not to take the shot personally, but it was hard. Especially when Christine Gardiner grimaced in agreement. Emma had worked alongside these women for years, and she knew them to be fair, nonjudgmental people. Of course, their dire outlook on the situation might have something to do with their sudden change of attitude toward her. For the first time she realized that she might not be up to the task she'd set for herself. But then her New Englander backbone asserted itself, and she looked each of them directly in the eyes before speaking in the calmest voice she could muster.

"I know you're both scared. I am, too. I've lived here my entire life, and I have no desire to leave Liberty Creek for another job somewhere else. I love my students, and just the thought of leaving them behind makes me want to cry."

The two older women traded guilty looks, and Dina frowned. "I apologize for being so tough on you. I'm just terrified of what's going to happen to Jerry and me if we lose my income. He's not as strong as he used to be when he was younger, and they just cut his hours at the factory again."

"It takes two jobs to keep a family afloat these days," Christine added somberly. "My music position was made part-time last year, and we're barely making ends meet as it is. We own our house, but if we have to move to find better jobs, who's going to want to buy a place in a town that's headed downhill?"

Emma's memory flashed to Rick's comment about visiting small towns that had all but disappeared from the map. Liberty Creek had been around for so long, she couldn't imagine it declining to the point of vanishing altogether. But she had to concede that economic theory wasn't her strong point. Calling up the optimism that had gotten her through endless rounds of chemo, she forced conviction into her tone.

"We're not going to let that happen here," she announced sternly as if being stubborn about it could somehow make it true. "We have to draw the line somewhere, and the school is an excellent place to start. Music and art aren't luxuries that can be cut when money gets tight. Creativity is an important part of every child's education, because it teaches them how to use their minds to do something other than parrot back facts to pass a test. There's nothing wrong with memorizing dates and formulas, but there's more involved in building productive adults."

"Like heart," Christine said, hope sparking in her eyes as she continued Emma's line of thought. "If kids don't learn to be compassionate and caring, we'll end up with a generation of robots."

"You're absolutely right." At the sound of Rick's voice, the three women whipped around to find him walking up behind them. Setting down his ever-present briefcase, he smiled as he took a seat beside Emma. "If you don't mind, Mrs. Gardiner, I'd like to use that line of yours about robots in our presentation to the school board next month."

Clearly flattered, she abandoned her wary expression and beamed at him. "Of course. If you think it will help."

"Everything will help," he assured her, including Dina with a practiced smile before sending a confident look around the anxious gathering. "But we all have to agree on our approach, or it won't work. I promise not to force any tactics on you that you don't approve of, if you'll promise to be open-minded about my suggestions. Deal?"

"Deal," Emma replied immediately. The other two exchanged a dubious look, but after a few hold-your-breath moments, they nodded their agreement.

"Excellent. Emma, I have a couple questions for you. Could I have a minute?"

She had a pretty good idea about what he'd be opening with, but she motioned him into the kitchen, hoping the gesture looked casual and unconcerned. When he reached the corner farthest from the buzzing crowd, he spread his hands with a baffled look. "What happened to this being just you and the two other teachers you mentioned?"

"Well, it started out that way," she confessed in a hushed voice, "but it kind of snowballed from there."

"I can see that. What I don't understand is why."

"Seriously?" she blurted before realizing that one of her favorite comebacks might come across as rude to him.

Fortunately, he grinned and nodded. "Seriously. Most people I've met don't pay much attention to what happens to anyone other than themselves."

"I think you've been living in the wrong kinds of places," Emma announced reflexively. "Around here, we care about what our neighbors are going through, and if we can lend a hand, we do. We don't wait for someone to come along and bail us out. We take care of problems ourselves."

"Is that a New England thing, or a Liberty Creek thing?"

"Both. And we're very proud of that," she clarified, just in case there was any question in his mind about what sort of people he was dealing with. Her hometown was peppered with quirky characters who didn't always get along, but when the chips were down, they'd do everything they could to help each other. In her mind, that quality was one of the best things about the map-dot town she'd grown up in.

"You should be," he said, running a hand through his hair as he stared at the arched opening between the living room and kitchen. "I don't have nearly enough printouts for everyone here tonight, and a lot of what I've put together is visual. Any suggestions?"

She considered the problem for a few moments before a suggestion popped into her head. "When Sam and Holly are working on a furniture project, sometimes they find plans online. They hook up her computer to the TV to enlarge the pictures and make them easier to see."

"You mean, with an HDMI cable?"

She had no clue what an HDMI cable was, but he seemed to think it would do the job, so she decided to go along. "Sure, do you have one of those in your fancy briefcase?"

"I have one of everything," he assured her with a chuckle. "Great idea."

Score one for the flaky dreamer, she thought with a flush of pride. "Thanks."

The two of them headed back to the crowd just in time to see Ellie's new bakery assistant framed in the screen door. Emma excused herself and went to greet the culinary cavalry. "Hi, Alyssa. Thanks so much for coming to my rescue."

"Your grandmother said it was an emergency," the slender young woman said as she followed Emma into the kitchen. She set an armload of white boxes imprinted in burgundy with *Ellie's Bakery and Bike Rentals* on the table. Glancing back through the doorway, she added, "I have to admit, I thought she was kidding about how urgent the situation was. I mean, I've never heard of solving a problem with pastry, but now I get it."

"I really appreciate you getting them here so fast. How are you enjoying your new job?"

"It's the best one I've had since…" She made a show of thinking it over, and then laughed. "Ever. I've only been there a couple of weeks, but I've learned a lot from Ellie, and she keeps letting me try new things whenever I think I'm ready. She keeps saying she should stop, though, so I don't learn enough from her to open my own place and put her out of business."

"That sounds like Gran," Emma said with a fond smile. "The truth is, you could learn everything she's ever known, and she'd still do it all better."

"I got that feeling, too. How does she manage that?"

"I have no idea. I'm hoping it's hereditary, though, and it'll make sense when I'm older."

"I'll have to do my best to soak it in on my own." When Emma offered her a tip, Alyssa put up her hands and backed away. "Not a chance. I've had a few bumps along the way to Liberty Creek, and I wasn't sure about coming here. People have been wonderful to me, so I'm happy to help out here and there. My aunt Frida lives here, and when she heard about my troubles, she insisted I come, at least for a visit."

"Frida's a sweetheart, that's for sure. How are things going for you now?"

"Much better," Alyssa confided on a sigh. "I was drowning on my own, and I had nowhere else to turn. Your grandmother wasn't officially hiring anyone new, but when she heard about my circumstances, she offered me a job. Considering all she's done for me, I'd take her desserts to the North Pole if she asked me to."

Emma wasn't sure what troubles Alyssa was referring to, but it didn't surprise her to learn that Gran had been doing more than just employing the new girl in town. There was no more generous person on the planet than Ellie Calhoun, she mused as she walked Alyssa to the front door. As the youngest in her family—and the only girl—she'd always enjoyed a special relationship with her adoring grandmother. She was elated to know that Gran's special touch was making a difference in the life of someone who so clearly needed a guardian angel.

In no time, she and some volunteers had refreshments for everyone, and they chatted while Rick reorganized his presentation. Once he finished connecting his laptop to her TV, he gave her a questioning look, and she nodded.

Referring to the printed version in his hand, he began. "I was able to get these budgetary figures from the board, and as you can see, they don't look very encouraging. The contingency fund is dangerously low, and half the school bus fleet is in serious need of either repair or replacement. Then there's the thirty-year-old roof at the elementary school."

"I need to bring in buckets for my classroom every time it rains," Dina complained. "Not to mention the flood we had in there when the snow that had piled up on the roof over the winter melted this spring."

"And the temperature variations are crazy," Christine said, shivering. "In January, it's freezing, and this time of year, we're melting."

"If you had computers in those rooms, it'd be different," the main office receptionist groused. "The offices and computer lab at the high school are like a freezer all year round, to keep the equipment from overheating. But we're just people, so we're forced to put up with it."

Rick was typing notes into his phone while they all stared at him, obviously waiting for a response. When the silence finally got through to him, he looked up. "Go ahead, folks. I'm just getting all this down."

"Maybe you should sit and listen for a while," Emma suggested as gently as she could. She was beginning to understand why some folks around town had formed the opinion that he was more interested in the bank's profits than their problems. "Sometimes when someone is typing, it gives people the impression that they're not paying attention."

Thankfully, he took the hint and put his phone facedown on a side table. Smiling, he held out his hands as if to show there was nothing in them anymore. "My apologies. Please go ahead."

"I'm thinking," one man chimed in, "that we don't need those new buses. What we need is to fix the ones we've got and use the money to keep our teachers."

"That makes a lot of sense," Rick told him in a sympathetic tone, "but school funds don't work that way. Money comes in from the state, earmarked for specific expense items, like maintenance, transportation and educational equipment. You can't shift the dollars around to suit yourself, no matter how good your intentions are."

"Why not?"

"Because those are the rules," Rick explained in a patient tone Emma assumed he'd perfected with his daughters. "Otherwise, the administration could build a golf course on the athletic fields and enjoy themselves."

The veteran teacher glowered at him. "You think that's funny, young man?"

To his credit, Rick didn't backpedal or stammer about trying to lighten the mood, which he'd apparently been trying to do. Instead, he faced the man squarely and said, "I apologize, sir. I realize this is a very serious matter for the entire town, and I shouldn't have made light of it that way. I meant no disrespect."

The scowl eased a bit, and the other man gave a stiff nod. "Apology accepted. Now, let's get back to work and figure out what we're going to do to save these good people's jobs."

Rick flashed Emma a relieved glance, and she sent him a muted smile that she hoped wouldn't arouse anyone's suspicions. The last thing either of them needed was to give the very active Liberty Creek rumor mill any material that might get exaggerated and eventually spin out of control.

Causing minor scandals had always been Brian's forte, not hers. And she had every intention of keeping it that way.

* * *

"Daddy, my new painting is over here," Caitlin told him excitedly, tugging him forward by one hand while Aubrey clung to the other and pulled him backward.

Rick felt like the rope in a tug-of-war between his daughters, and he stopped with a laugh. "Hang on, Cait. Aubrey's legs are shorter than ours." He knew full well that wasn't the reason she was dragging her feet, but he didn't want her to know he realized that she was frightened of the large, noisy crowd that had come to school for the Liberty Creek art classes' annual open house. Timid on a good day, his shy girl found this kind of event terrifying, and he wished—again—that there was something he could do to make her feel more comfortable in these situations. As she grew older, there would be more of them, and so far, nothing he'd tried had worked. All he could really do was hope that she outgrew her aversion to unfamiliar people and places.

And then from the sea of faces emerged one that both of his girls had come to adore. Now that he thought about it, he amended with a grin to himself, he'd grown pretty fond of it himself.

"Hello, Marshalls," Emma greeted them,

pulling the girls into a hug before dazzling him with one of her incredible smiles. "This is a big night for our talented artists. I'm so glad you could all make it to the show."

"We wouldn't miss it for anything," Rick assured her, smiling back because he hadn't yet discovered a way to refrain from returning Emma's friendly gestures. He'd tried very hard to keep the enchanting teacher at a distance, but he was a guy, and it was beginning to dawn on him that it might be impossible for him to resist her. The fact that she was such a wonderful influence on his daughters didn't escape him, and that only made it more difficult to maintain his characteristic reserve.

Part of him didn't even want to, and he reluctantly acknowledged that the ratio was growing every day. Like one of his pie charts, he realized with a mental groan, where one section kept increasing its percentage of the whole no matter what strategy he employed to bring it back in line with the rest of his numbers. But his feelings weren't like money management, and he could definitely do something about them. The trouble was, he didn't know what was causing his emotions to run away with him, so he wasn't sure what that "something" might be.

He came back to earth when he noticed that the three ladies he was standing with were all staring at him, apparently waiting for him to respond to whatever they were talking about. Feeling like a moron, he shook his head and chuckled. "Sorry about that. You lost me for a second. What were you saying?"

"That us girls like pink and purple," Aubrey explained, pointing to the three in the group, "but boys like different colors. What colors do you like?"

"Blue's my favorite, but I like green, too."

"What kind of blue?" Caitlin prodded. "There are lots of different ones."

"I don't know," he hedged, looking to Emma for some assistance. Her feminine smirk told him that he was on his own, but he drew inspiration from the pretty artist's features. "The color of a clear sky is nice. Especially when you're on a sailboat, relaxing and enjoying the day."

"Interesting," she commented, the smug look warming into a dreamy one. "I've never been sailing, but I've always wanted to try it."

"It's like flying," Aubrey told her, holding her arms out and rocking in a very untimid motion. "We've been on a plane, but sailing is way more fun. You can feel the wind, and the sun is really warm."

"And then you get a sunburn," Caitlin added in a big-sister tone. "Remember?"

"It was still fun."

"Where did you go sailing?" Emma asked, clearly fascinated by the experience. Somehow, she managed to address her question to the entire family, and once more Rick was amazed by her ability to include all of them in a conversation. Then it struck him: she didn't talk down to his daughters. They were young enough that most adults spoke to them in much simpler terms than were necessary. Condescending, almost.

But not Emma. He supposed it was because she was so accustomed to dealing with children of all ages, and she assessed each one as an individual rather than assuming that they were all alike. She'd done that with him, too, he recognized, giving him a chance to prove what kind of man he was instead of jumping to conclusions about him the way so many people seemed to do.

"Myrtle Beach," he replied, smiling at the memory. "Last summer the girls and I met up with my parents and some relatives I hadn't seen in a while. Our kids are all around the same age, so they had a lot of fun playing on the beach. We rented a sailboat one day and took it out for a few hours. I hadn't sailed in years, but my uncle and I managed to get everyone back in one piece."

"Uncle Gene is the best!" Caitlin announced, eyes shining affectionately. "He let us kids steer the boat and everything."

Gene had only turned the wheel over to the rug rats when there was absolutely nothing for them to run into, but Rick kept that detail to himself. It had been the first trip they'd taken since losing Sarah, and there was no way he'd spoil that wonderful memory with reality. His girls had gotten enough of that to last them a long, long time.

"Maybe sometime you can teach me how to do that," Emma suggested. "But for now, I'm thinking that your dad came by tonight to see your artwork."

She gave Aubrey a quick wink before leading them to the display, and Rick wondered what the two of them were keeping from him. It was a new experience for him to feel like the odd guy out, and he wasn't too proud to admit that it bothered him. He'd often wished that his daughters had a woman close by that they could giggle and share secrets with, but he'd gladly stepped into that role because there was no one else for them. Mrs. Fields was a warm, affectionate presence in their lives, but she was a nanny to them, not a friend.

Now they had a more personal feminine influence, and he wasn't sure how he felt about being replaced as their confidante.

Long tables arranged throughout the gym held everything from lopsided pottery to animal portraits to an Eiffel Tower made entirely of popsicle sticks. Rick paused in front of it, saying, "Now, I've seen the real thing, and I have to say I'm impressed. This is fantastic."

"One of my middle-schoolers did that," Emma informed him proudly. "It took him most of the past month, and yesterday we were blasting the glue with a cool hair dryer to make sure it was completely solid. I didn't want it to fall apart on its way here."

Rick loved the pride she felt in her student's success, and it occurred to him that it wasn't the first time he'd heard her speak about one of her pupils that way. She genuinely cared about them, doing everything she could to support them in reaching their goals. That was the kind of teacher every kid deserved, and he hoped—again—that their efforts to save her job wouldn't be in vain. Losing Emma would be a huge blow to her students and eventually the quaint village itself. That was how small towns began to lose their identity, he knew, as small school districts merged to cut expenses and gradually the town governments followed suit.

In his mind, Liberty Creek's greatest assets were the residents who were dedicated to maintaining the independent spirit that had founded the place many of the families had called home for generations. Unfortunately, at some point reality had to become part of the equation, and tough decisions would have to be made. He only hoped that this charming New Hampshire village would survive its latest challenge and continue to exist in the same self-reliant way it had since its founding.

On the far side of the gym, Emma stopped and let Aubrey lead them toward a spot on the wall that held a small handwritten label with her name on it. Since she wasn't a student yet, he knew that Emma must have approved her participation and cleared a spot for her to use.

Turning to Emma, he murmured, "Thanks for letting her do this."

"Caitlin asked me if she could put up something that Aubrey drew, and I couldn't say no," the softhearted teacher told him with a smile.

"I haven't seen it yet, so it will be a surprise to me, too. I have to admit, your daughters are impossible to resist."

"Tell me about it," he commented, chuckling. When he got closer to the crayon portrait, his amusement shifted to confusion. Hunkering down to his younger girl's level, he said, "I like your drawing, sweetness, but I'm not sure what's going on there. Can you explain it to me?"

From the corner of his eye he noticed Emma's baffled expression, but he ignored that to focus on Aubrey. Eyes sparkling enthusiastically, she explained, "That's you, me, Caitlin and Emma at the playground after our first day at church. The angel looking down from heaven is Mommy."

He'd seen all of her drawings from the time she could hold a crayon. Kittens, puppies, unicorns, she'd drawn every animal ever conceived—both real and fictional—and many sketches of the family doing various activities together. She'd never included anyone else, and he was bewildered about why she'd be doing it now. Concerned about her emotional state, he gently asked, "Why did you draw Mommy?"

"You said she's always watching us," Aubrey pointed out as if it should have been obvious.

"I think she's glad that we like doing things with Emma."

"You mean, you and Caitlin enjoy Emma's company?"

"So do you, Daddy," she corrected him sweetly. "You smile a lot when she's around. I think Mommy likes that, because she wants you to be happy. Being happy is important."

He couldn't argue with her logic, mostly because he recognized that she had a point. Reaching out, he pulled her into a quick hug before letting go. "You know what? I think you're right."

Rick stood and gave Emma an apologetic look. "Sorry about this. It must be kind of awkward seeing yourself in that picture."

Uncertainty dimmed her eyes, but was quickly chased off by her characteristic optimism. "A little, but it's also very thoughtful of you, Aubrey. Thank you."

"You're welcome. I had fun with everyone that day."

"So did I," Emma replied. "It was a perfect Sunday kind of afternoon."

"You can keep the picture if you want."

"Are you sure? You must have worked pretty hard to get it just right." When Aubrey nodded,

Emma said, "Then thank you again. I have exactly the right-sized frame for it at home."

"You're gonna put it in a frame?" Caitlin asked, clearly amazed.

"I do that with all my favorite pieces. Maybe you girls would like to come over and help me find the right place to hang it."

"And have some of Grandma Ellie's cookies?" Aubrey prodded, eyes lighting in anticipation.

"Sure. Which ones do you want?"

The girls each shouted out different varieties, and Emma laughed. "I'm not sure which ones I have, but we can probably find something from your list. In the meantime, maybe we should keep going and see the other projects here tonight. The kids put a lot of effort into their projects, and I'd like to see how they all turned out."

She held out her hands, and the girls each grabbed one, pulling her forward, with Rick trailing behind them. While they chattered their way through the displays, he found himself admiring the way Emma managed to talk to all of them at once, making sure none of them felt ignored.

In a quieter moment, he felt that old light touch on his shoulder, a quick brush of warmth against his cheek as if someone had kissed him. And just as quickly as it had appeared, it was gone.

At eight, the show was over, and Emma walked them toward the door. "Thanks so much for coming. The students really love showing off their work, so it's great when so many people come by to see what they've been doing."

"Aren't you leaving, too?" Rick asked.

"Not yet. The custodians take care of the heavy stuff, but I want to get the art safely back to my room before I go. These things are precious, and I'd hate to see anything get lost or damaged."

Hearing her describe the children's artwork as if they were priceless masterpieces touched him in a way that was strange and pleasant all at once. So much of his day was spent valuing portfolios and assessing financial risks that he sometimes lost sight of the fact that there were things in the world so valuable you couldn't put a price on them. Grateful to her for reminding him of that, he offered, "We can help if you want. It'll go faster that way."

The girls were only too eager to extend their time with Emma, so the job went quickly and without mishap. Once all the treasures had been safely stowed in Emma's room, she slid Aubrey's portrait into a small leather folder and handed it to the artist. Then she locked the door and turned to them with an invitation gleaming in her eyes. "Who wants cookies?"

Squealing in delight, his daughters nearly squashed her in a joyful embrace and all but danced their way out of the school. Following after them, she flashed Rick an apologetic look. "Sorry. I should've asked you first. You probably have work to do."

He did, actually. He always did. But tonight it was the furthest thing from his mind. "Nothing that can't wait."

"It's a beautiful night for a walk," she went on, tilting her head back for a look into a sky glimmering with stars. Bright as they were, they still couldn't compare with her sparkling eyes.

Rick had never met an adult who found such joy in simple, everyday occurrences, and before he realized what was happening, he heard himself saying, "It's great how you appreciate the little things."

Turning those incredible eyes on him, she studied him with an unreadable look. Then, offering a hint of a smile, she said, "When you've been through what I have, the little things become the big things."

"I can relate to that."

But for the first time he could remember, it didn't make him sad. Instead, he felt a kinship with this sweet, strong woman who'd emerged from her ordeal and popped into his life for some reason he still didn't understand. But lately, he'd begun wondering if the God that he'd never given much thought to had brought him here to this out-of-the-way place on purpose. What that purpose might be had eluded him until tonight, when his four-year-old so wisely reminded him that being happy was important.

He was trying to come up with a way to express that to Emma when they reached her front yard, and the girls raced up the steps to the porch. Putting his baffling emotions on hold for now, he called out, "Hold on, girls. This isn't our house."

"Oh, go on in," Emma contradicted him, beeping the lock open with the remote she held. "Cookies are in the jar on the table."

Following at a slower pace, he angled his head for a closer look at the gizmo in her hand. "I didn't realize you were so techie."

"I'm not," she replied, laughing again. "Sam insisted on installing an alarm system, and this is how you make it work. I was fine using the old key and lock, but big brother wasn't satisfied, so last week he came by to put in this system for me. Calhoun boys are very stubborn, so when one of them gets an idea in his head, it's better just to go along."

Rick couldn't hold back a grin. "Funny, that's what they say about you."

She cocked one disapproving eyebrow, but the gesture was muted by the sisterly affection twinkling in her eyes. "I'm sure."

"So, this church improvement project I've signed myself up for," he went on while they went up the stairs into her chaotic, cheery living room. "Do you do this kind of thing very often?"

"Every year it's something different. The chapel has been around since 1821, so it needs a lot of TLC. Coffee?"

"Sure, thanks." In no time, he was enjoying a homemade latte and one of Ellie's delicious orange scones. "This is nice. Feeding people well must run in the family."

"I wish," Emma replied with a bright laugh. "I'm good at heating things up and arranging them on a plate to make them look nice, but that's where it ends for me. Most of the time, I get involved in my latest creation and forget I have something in the oven. It's much safer for everyone if I let Mom and Gran do the cooking."

"Everyone has their talents," Rick commented. "Mine is numbers."

"And being a great daddy," Caitlin reminded him in between bites of her cookie.

"The best one ever," Aubrey added earnestly, blue eyes shining in the light from the vintage chandelier that hung over Emma's kitchen table.

Rick still wasn't sure what he'd done to deserve such amazing children, but he was grateful for them every single day. "Well, that's what my mug says, right?"

"It's not easy being a parent, that's for sure," Emma said. "When I see my brothers with their kids, I realize how tough a job it can be."

"Comes with lots of perks, though. Plenty of hugs and pajama days, and cereal in bed on Father's Day. Not to mention seeing your kids growing up and turning into good people." Sending a look from one daughter to the other, he smiled. "You always make me proud to be your father."

"And we're proud to be your girls," Caitlin informed him, while Aubrey nodded her agreement.

"That's so sweet," Emma said as she got to her feet. Reaching in from behind, she gave them a quick group hug. "You two are the absolute best, you know that?"

"You are, too, Emma," Aubrey said without a bit of her usual shyness. "We think you're awesome."

"Well, thank you! That calls for another squeeze." This one was a little tighter, and they both squealed in surprise before dissolving into a fit of giggles, which Emma joined them in. Rick leaned back in his chair, savoring the sweet moment with a lightness in his heart that he hadn't felt in ages. And that was when he knew.

Despite his best efforts, he was in real danger of falling for Emma Calhoun. For her pixie looks and her indomitable spirit and her kind, open heart. She'd given so much to him and his daughters in the short time they'd known her, and somehow, without him noticing, he'd returned the feelings.

He wasn't quite certain how that had happened, but it occurred to him that anyone walking past one of the oversize windows would assume that they were a family enjoying an evening snack together.

Hoping to mask his sudden discomfort, he stood and clapped his hands together. "We came to help Emma find a spot to display Aubrey's picture. It's a school night, so we should do that and get home."

"Hang on," Emma said. "I'll go get the frame I want to use."

Once she had it, she quickly tucked the print inside and held it up for them to see. Then, glancing from Caitlin to Aubrey, she gave them a playful look and said, "Three-two-one—go!"

The girls jumped right to it, hurrying from one place to the next, trying the portrait in several spots before settling on the last place he would have expected.

"How about up there?" Caitlin asked, pointing to the hand-hewn mantel over the arched brick fireplace.

It was already overloaded with family photos, and Rick shook his head. "It's pretty crowded up there, Cait. Why don't you find someplace else?"

"Oh, that's no big deal," Emma assured him, waving off his suggestion as she went over to the fireplace. Sliding a few frames aside, she set Aubrey's picture front and center. Then she stepped back to assess the effect and nodded. "I think that's perfect. Does it work for the artist?"

Aubrey's face broke into a delighted smile, and it was clear that she was thrilled to be referred to in such grown-up terms. "It looks really nice there."

"Now when I get home every day, it's the first thing I'll notice. And I'm sure my guests will want to hear all about who drew it."

"Really?" Aubrey asked, eyes shining at the thought. "That would be cool."

"Very," Emma agreed, pulling her into a hug. "Thank you so much for giving it to me."

"You're welcome."

Rick figured this was a good opportunity to get them heading toward the door. Whenever they visited Emma, he needed a crowbar to pry them away from her. Ordinarily, he didn't mind that much, but his reaction to her earlier had put him more on edge than usual.

On the way home, the girls chattered excitedly about their evening and how much fun they'd all had. Rick didn't need to do more than comment here and there, and the cheerful talk continued right through tuck-in time.

Following that, the house fell quiet, giving

him time to reflect on what was bothering him all of a sudden. Unfortunately, he came up with the same explanation he had earlier, and he wasn't sure how he felt about it.

Not only was pursuing a romantic relationship with Emma not even remotely in his plans, it also went against the most important thing that he'd promised himself he would never do: get involved with a woman who had cancer. She appeared to be healthy now, but he knew only too well how abruptly that could change. For a man who spent his days devising ways to avoid risk, opening himself up to so much of it went against his nature. He enjoyed spending time with Emma, and the girls had made it clear that they adored her. That was where it had to stop, for all their sakes.

Satisfied with his decision—again—he settled into bed and closed his eyes. As he drifted off to sleep, he heard Emma's unmistakable laughter ringing through his memory and sighed. There was no point in denying it. The bright, sassy art teacher had found a way around his well-honed defenses and was threatening to collapse them altogether.

But that didn't mean he had to give in and let it happen.

Chapter Seven

It's not every day that a retired movie star asks you over to her beautiful home for lunch.

Especially when you both live in a tiny town like Liberty Creek, Emma added silently as she turned onto a wide lane that led to a graceful circular drive. The dark gray color told her everything had recently been paved, and she recalled how the path used to be nothing but dirt and weeds poking up through a thin layer of gravel. The dilapidated house that used to stand here was gone, replaced by a grand Colonial with an expansive front porch and wings out to either side of the enormous double oak doors that beckoned visitors to come inside.

Sam's largest rehab project to date, he referred to it as his pride and joy. The woman who lived there had given him a purpose when he'd needed one, and her daughter had shown the good sense to look beyond Sam's reserved manner to the wonderful heart that beat so steadily beneath it. Emma would always be grateful to both of them for helping her beloved older brother rediscover the happiness life could bring.

Affectionately referred by her family as "The Diva," Daphne Mills glided out onto the porch and extended her arms in a welcoming gesture. Dressed in the casual elegance that had been her style during her Hollywood career, Emma knew that the sparkling rings and bracelet she wore were the real McCoy. But all those gems couldn't match the delight shining in those famous violet eyes.

After embracing Emma warmly, Daphne stepped back and beamed at her. "You look wonderful. Are you counting the days until you get your summer vacation?"

She summoned a smile that she didn't quite feel. "Summer's the best time for painting, so I always find plenty of ways to enjoy it."

The older woman eyed her suspiciously before putting an arm around her shoulders for a quick squeeze. In the trademark Southern accent that gave her so much of her charm, she said, "You're a terrible actress, honey. You don't have to keep up that brave front when you're with me. I've been through more jobs than you can shake a stick at, and I know how hard it is waiting to hear about one that you want more than anything. Now, come in and tell me all about what you've been up to lately."

She'd known Daphne for over a year now, but it still felt weird to be talking to the former film star as if they were two regular people chatting with each other. Gracious and engaging, she made Emma feel like the most important visitor she'd ever had. Where she got all that self-assurance from baffled Emma, but then she recalled the grit Holly had shown from the moment she'd come to town with her son, Chase, determined to make a better life for them both. Apparently, confidence was a Mills family trait.

Just like it was for her brothers and so many other Calhouns, Emma mused with a mental sigh. She just wished she'd inherited more of it. While she and Daphne traded news, Emma wondered again about the invitation. It had come from out of the blue, and while the two of them weren't strangers, they'd never gotten together just the two of them until now. She couldn't shake the feeling that Daphne had suggested this lunch for a reason that had noth-

ing to do with finger sandwiches and freshly
brewed iced tea.

"You and Holly just got back from Paris,"
Emma said at one point. "Did you girls have
some wild adventures?"

Laughing brightly, Daphne pantomimed
turning a lock on her lips and tossing away the
key. Then she winked and added more sugar
to her drink. "You folks up here haven't quite
figured out this cold tea idea. No matter what
I tell people, they never make it sweet enough
for me."

Emma wasn't sure what to say, so she just
smiled and sipped her own, which was perfectly sugared for her taste. After a bite of a
sandwich, Daphne swallowed and sat back,
crossing one silk pant leg over the other. Giving Emma a thoughtful look, she finally got
down to business. "When I'm in Paris, I always
visit the Louvre and marvel at all the fabulous
artwork they have inside those walls. During
this trip, I had a thought."

"About?"

"You. Specifically, your job situation. Would
you rather I didn't interfere, or are you interested in hearing it?"

"Very interested," Emma replied, leaning
forward eagerly. This woman had crafted a

long, successful career in the most cutthroat business on earth outside of politics. If Daphne had some insight for her, she was more than open to suggestions.

"Well, I noticed several groups of school children at the Louvre, all in their matching uniforms, listening to one of the docents drone on about something or other. My French isn't the best, but I could pick up one thing—they were bored out of their little skulls. Art isn't for talking about. It's for experiencing firsthand, getting your fingers dirty or full of paint while you create something out of thin air. Would you agree?"

"Wholeheartedly. When we were growing up, Granddad always told us that the best way to learn is to try and fail, then pick yourself up and try again. When you learn how not to do something, you're one step closer to figuring out how to succeed."

Approval twinkled in Daphne's eyes. "A wise man. Sam and Brian quote him like that all the time. I wish I could have met him."

"You would've liked each other," Emma commented with a smile, glancing around the sunroom that Sam had restored to its original glory. "He always loved this old place, and he'd be happy knowing that you liked it well enough to bring it back to life."

"I'm glad to hear that. Now, back to your problem. I have an idea for you."

Daphne motioned around her in a sweeping, dramatic gesture reminiscent of the screen persona she'd cultivated during her long career. "You and I have discussed my art collection many times, because we have the same fondness for the Impressionists. Your work has the same soft, dreamy quality of Monet and Degas, and I know from talking to Chase that you encourage your students to interpret the world around them in their own unique ways. You're the kind of teacher I want for my grandson, and for all the other children in our school."

"That's very flattering, and I really appreciate your support of me," Emma said, still curious about where this was heading. "What did you have in mind?"

"The Daphne Mills Fine Arts Department," she responded, holding up her hand and moving it slowly through the air as if she was tracing the lettering on an invisible sign. Then she met Emma's eyes intently. "I'll provide the funding, you provide the expertise. You and the music teachers keep your jobs, and the kids keep three of their favorite teachers. It's a win-win."

Clearly, this woman had more than a little experience with negotiating, while Emma felt very much out of her element. Taking a moment to let the burst of excitement subside, she toyed with her spoon to pull her thoughts together. Keenly aware that her potential fairy godmother's feelings could be easily hurt, she started simply. "Daphne, that's incredibly generous of you."

"Practical, you mean. We have a problem at the school, and this is an obvious solution. Frankly, I'm disappointed that you and Rick didn't approach me about it sooner. I had to hear about it through the grapevine."

Her forehead knit into an expression that told Emma she was being honest about her disappointment, and Emma quickly said, "Honestly, it didn't occur to us." She wasn't actually sure about Rick, but she forged ahead, anyway. "From what I gather, your proposal—wonderful as it is—can't be accomplished at a public school. Our funding comes from the state, with money specifically targeted to certain areas."

"That's absurd," Daphne spat, eyes flaring indignantly. "Every sports event I go to does fund-raising for their kids. Those are school-sponsored teams."

"The money goes to the booster club, and they use it for the team's benefit," Emma explained calmly. "That's different."

Clearly flustered by the obstacle, Daphne fumed for several moments before announcing, "So we need an arts department booster club."

"That would be great, but the school year's almost over, so we can't accomplish much now. Even if it was earlier in the year, any money we'd be able to earn wouldn't make up the shortfall." Pausing for breath, she went on sadly. "I might be able to help out by going to part-time, but I'm still paying off college loans and some pretty steep medical bills. I can't afford that kind of hit to my salary."

"Meaning you have to work full-time, either here or somewhere else."

"Exactly. But I'm very grateful to you for trying to help, Daphne."

"If only there was something I could do." Sitting back again, Daphne tapped the rim of her glass with a perfectly manicured coral nail. Something lit her eyes, and she smiled across the bistro table at Emma. "What if I sponsor your after-school arts program? At least that way, the kids will have a creative outlet, even if they won't have an official art class anymore."

Overjoyed, Emma impulsively leaped from her chair and hugged her. She didn't often do things like that, and when she regained her senses, she quickly pulled away. "I'm sorry. Did I crush you?"

"Yes, but there's no harm done. From your enthusiasm, can I assume that you'd like to take me up on my offer?"

"Absolutely," Emma gushed, returning to her seat wearing a grin so big, she could almost see it herself. "I'm just not sure how to set it up properly."

"I'm sure Rick can help us with that," Daphne announced confidently, waving a regal hand as if that was enough to make it happen. "From what I've heard, he's good with numbers and isn't averse to bending the rules to benefit people he cares about."

Emma got the impression that Daphne had acquired some bad intel from the town's active gossip chain and hastily set her straight. "There's nothing special going on between Rick and me. We're just working together on this school issue, that's all."

"Nothing special," Daphne repeated, arching one expertly sculpted brow in obvious disagreement. "Are you sure about that?"

"Completely."

That response got her a dubious head tilt, and Emma fought the urge to squirm. She managed to keep her cool, though, and was relieved when Daphne shifted topics to the recent art show and what kinds of projects the students had put on display.

Their conversation was light and casual, similar to others they'd had in the past, and Emma was thankful to have the spotlight off her private life. Not that she had anything to hide where Rick Marshall was concerned. He'd made it clear that he wasn't interested in having anything more with her than sharing the occasional walk around town or dinner with his girls. Especially considering how much he'd been through with his late wife's cancer, she was content with having him as just a friend.

But now that Daphne had suggested that he might be feeling something more for her, Emma couldn't help wondering if she was right.

When Rick showed up for paint duty on Saturday afternoon, the contractor in charge gave him a long, doubtful stare. His work clothes weren't covered in paint and grease like the others, so he could understand the man's concern. "I did this kind of work all through college. I promise you, I know what I'm doing."

Still unconvinced, Roger dipped an angled brush into a small can of trim color and handed it to him, handle first. "All right, then. Show me what ya got."

Rick smothered a grin as he chose a section of window trim that had been primed but was still missing its final coat. Working carefully but quickly, he laid down a perfect line of white that stood out from the faded paint around it. He worked his way along the sill, encouraged by the fact that Roger didn't tell him to stop. Bolstered by the man's unspoken approval, he kept going until he reached the other side.

Turning, he reminded himself not to sound too eager. "Whattya think?"

The painter strolled along, leaning in to study Rick's work as if it was being considered for a museum. Meeting Rick's eyes in the direct New Englander manner that signified respect, he nodded. "It'll do."

Without another comment, he turned on the heel of a paint-spattered boot and strode across the sanctuary to oversee the crew patching the old plasterwork on the other wall.

"Don't take it too hard, Rick," a familiar voice said as a hand came down on his shoulder from behind. "He made his own son apply for an open job last year, and the kid's been working in the business since he was ten."

Glancing back, he saw Brian Calhoun grinning at him.

"My father's like that, too," Rick informed him with a grin of his own. "He likes to say that family is family, and business is business. He doesn't approve of mixing the two, which is why I work for a different bank."

"Huh. Guess we're the opposite. Grandad gave Dad his first job out of high school, and Sam and I love working together."

"We do?" the oldest Calhoun growled as he joined them. Rick and Brian were both about six feet tall, but the former Army Ranger towered over them both. Rick had learned that Sam was a gentle giant, but he didn't mind admitting that being around a guy built like an oak tree was a little intimidating.

"Sure, we do. With Jordan coming on board soon, it'll be great. And profitable," Brian added, obviously for Rick's benefit.

"You can save that kind of talk for my office," Rick told him, chuckling. "Today I'm just here to help spruce up the church, like everyone else."

Neither of the Calhouns seemed to be in a hurry to get to work, and while they traded small talk, his instincts warned him that there was something unusual going on. Figuring it was up to them to bring up whatever was on their minds, he kept up his end of the light-hearted conversation, waiting for them to finally get to the point.

Before they had a chance, Emma sailed over, carrying a large tray full of snacks and lemonade. "Hello there, boys. Can I interest you in something sweet?"

"Always," Brian answered, helping himself. Sam didn't respond, and a quick glance over showed Rick that the contractor was eyeing him intently. More reserved than his younger brother, Sam's expression didn't give Rick even the slightest hint about what he might be thinking. And in Rick's experience, that was usually a bad thing.

Smiling up at Rick, Emma leaned in and whispered, "There's some snickerdoodles under that plate. I saved them for you."

Returning her smile was a simple thing, and he didn't bother trying to play it cool in front of her brothers. After taking a cup of lemonade, he thanked her and took a bite that just about melted in his mouth. "These are fantastic. Tell Ellie I said thank you."

Her cheeks pinked a bit, and she gave him a shy smile. "Actually, I made them."

"You did not," Brian scoffed, looking at her as if she'd grown an extra head.

"Well, they're Gran's recipe, but I baked them myself. This is the fourth batch."

"What happened to the first three?" he asked. When she remained silent, he laughed. "Enough said. Congrats, Emmy. You're officially no longer a hazard in the kitchen."

"Be nice and maybe I'll learn how to make ginger snaps for you."

He contemplated her offer for a few seconds and then shook his head, mischief twinkling in his eyes. "Think I'll play it safe and pass."

Letting out an exasperated breath, she stuck her tongue out at him and went off in a huff that was plainly more drama than serious.

"Why'd you do that?" Sam demanded. "She worked hard on those cookies, and you hurt her feelings."

"I treated her like I always do, instead of like someone who needs to be handled with kid gloves," Brian reminded him in a quiet voice. "Like I did with you when you came home from the service."

After a quiet moment Sam nodded. Normally, Rick would have felt awkward being part of what should have been a family moment, but for some reason he didn't. It occurred to him that it was because the Calhouns apparently thought of him as more than an acquaintance.

Before he could pursue that thought, Sam cleared his throat and said, "We'd like to talk to you for a minute."

Rick followed them to an alcove away from the bustling crew in the chapel. When they were in relative privacy, Emma's older brothers stopped and turned to face him squarely. Their arms were folded, their faces set in comparable stony lines like two old-time gunfighters. If it hadn't been him in the line of fire, it might've been funny.

Since he was the oldest, Sam went first. "We're wondering—like a lot of folks in town—what's going on with you and Emma?"

"Don't beat around the bush, Sam," Rick joked. "Tell me what's bothering you." Those looks went from stony to concrete, and he regretted trying to lighten the mood. "Sorry about that. I know you're concerned about who she gets involved with, but we're just friends."

Brian made a derisive noise, narrowing his eyes in disbelief. "Not a chance. Lindsay and I were 'just friends,' and look where we ended up."

"We're not you and Lindsay."

"You spend an awful lotta time together," Sam pointed out.

"Working on joint projects," Rick insisted in an equally reasonable voice. "We have different strengths, and we complement each other. In a professional way," he added quickly, just to be absolutely clear. Somehow, these two had gotten the idea that he was romantically interested in Emma, which couldn't be further from the truth.

Sure, he enjoyed spending time with her. Listening to the amusing details of her days, which were so unlike his own. Watching her eyes sparkle while she shared the inspiration for her latest artwork. Who wouldn't?

"She has dinner at your house almost every night," Brian pointed out.

"That doesn't mean anything. She has to eat somewhere, and my daughters love having her around."

"What about you?" Sam asked in a voice so

quiet that Rick had to strain to hear him over the background noise in the chapel.

He'd never been grilled this way, and while he understood their apprehension, he was just about done with their third degree. "I appreciate her company, and I assume she feels the same about me. But I promise you, that's all it is."

"Then you're a moron," Brian spat, apparently done with the subtle approach. "Emma's an amazing person, and if you're not interested in getting serious with her, then you're not half as smart as I thought you were."

The criticism stung, and Rick took a breath to cool his rising temper before speaking. "I have my reasons for not getting involved with Emma that way. *Personal* reasons."

"That's fine," Sam conceded somberly. "But do her a favor."

"What's that?"

"Take off your wedding ring," he growled, nodding in the direction of Rick's left hand. "Folks're starting to talk."

With that, he stalked from the alcove with Brian close behind.

Watching them go, Rick bristled at the menacing order he'd just received. After he'd cooled down a little and thought about it again, he realized that Sam had a point—and every right to protect his sister from the sort of gossip that might affect her reputation. She was a teacher, after all, and while she had a right to a personal life, he recognized that in a small town like this, the parents of her students held her to a higher moral standard than most.

His own indecisiveness about her bobbed to the surface of his mind, and he questioned the wisdom of continuing to pretend that he wasn't tempted to find out where those tentative steps might lead.

The choice he faced was obvious: he could either stay away from Emma completely or stop waffling and start dating her. The first option was a definite no, which left him with the second. Of course, it wasn't his decision alone. If she wanted to remain friends, that would end his internal debate once and for all. But if she didn't…

He'd never know until he asked. The trouble was, he hadn't dated anyone other than Sarah since meeting her during his freshman year of college. While he wasn't normally lacking for confidence, when it came to women, he didn't have much experience. But this was Emma, and he'd told her so many things already, this shouldn't be too hard.

Still, as he set out to find her, his stomach knotted in the kind of uneasiness he didn't suffer from often enough to understand it. Losing his nerve wasn't like him, and he gave himself a stiff mental shake to keep from chickening out.

From up ahead, he heard her laughing at something, and all his doubts vanished. Just the sound of it made him smile.

"Look at you!" Emma teased Rick when he came over to get a bottle of water from the refreshment table. "Did they finally decide to let you paint?"

"Yes, but we've got a few jokesters on the crew," he explained, turning to show her the white handprint on the back of his dark blue T-shirt.

"Oh, that's awful. They ruined that shirt."

"It was Brian."

"Why am I not surprised?" she said, shaking her head in mock disapproval. "I have to say, though, I like this look much better than what you normally wear."

She couldn't believe she'd said that out loud, and started busily rearranging fruit on a tray to avoid his gaze. Flirting wasn't her style, and she could feel her cheeks heating in embarrassment.

"Really?" She peeked up and saw male interest gleaming in his eyes as he edged a little closer. "Why is that?"

At first, all she could focus on was that glint of fascination, and her brain ground to a screeching halt. Locked in his intense gaze, she blinked twice in an attempt to regain her bearings. Finally, reason kicked in and she dragged her eyes away, but it wasn't easy.

"You look more comfortable." Could she sound any lamer? she chided herself in disgust. But she'd chosen that route, and she decided that it was best to stick with it for as long as she could manage it.

"I am, actually." Swallowing some water, he looked across the park to where his daughters were romping around the playground with some of the other volunteers' kids. Coming back to her, he continued, "It's not just the clothes, though. This whole community thing is a new experience for the girls and me. They really like it here."

"What about you?" she blurted without thinking. That was twice now, she moaned silently. She wasn't used to thinking about everything she said before she spoke, but apparently her mouth couldn't be trusted to run the show anymore. Then again, Rick didn't seem to mind the personal angle of their conversation. That was some consolation at least.

"I like it, too. Especially the people."

He added one of those artless grins very unlike the practiced smile he'd used when they first met. She'd come to understand that some of his expressions were reserved for people he trusted to see a bit more of him than he shared with others. Emma felt honored to be someone he felt relaxed enough with to be himself.

"That's nice to hear. We like you, too." When he tipped his head in a chiding gesture, she laughed. "Well, some of us do. Just give the rest some time. Once they get to know you, they'll come around."

"How do you know they're not right about me?"

"Because I do. We'd barely met when you offered to help with my presentation and then the effort to save our teaching jobs. That's not the kind of thing a heartless shark does."

"'Heartless shark,'" he echoed pensively. "That's a new one."

"And totally untrue," she hastened to add, her cheeks flaming again. "I can't believe I repeated that to you. I'm so sorry."

"Not your fault. In my business, you don't

make a lot of friends, and you get used to folks hating you when things don't go their way."

"No one *hates* you," she assured him. "They might hate some of the decisions you've made, but not you personally. People here aren't like that."

"You honestly believe that, don't you?"

"Yes, I do."

Eyeing her somberly, he studied her for several long, uncomfortable moments. Then, as if something in his attitude had suddenly shifted, he slowly nodded. "Then I believe it, too. I've lived in a lot of places, but I have to admit, Liberty Creek seems to be different from all of them. Somehow, you've managed to keep the character of this town from changing too much. Once you get used to it, it's kinda nice."

A slight tinge of the South had crept into his voice, and she smiled. "You sounded like Holly just then."

"Now, that's a downright insult," he teased, thickening the accent into a deeper drawl. "She's from Savannah. I'm from Charleston."

Emma laughed at the mock outrage.

He laughed before polishing off his water and tossing the empty bottle into a nearby recycling bin. Turning back to her, he said, "I guess it's because I feel like I can be myself with you. Usually, I smooth it down because in college they taught us that a flat accent sounds more professional. When it's just the two of us, I don't worry about all that."

She liked the way that sounded, and she couldn't help flirting just a little. "That seems dangerously like a compliment."

"Good, 'cause that's how I meant it." He paused as if there was something more he wanted to say to her. "I was wondering…"

"About what?"

"If there's a nice restaurant around here for dinner."

"That depends. Family or romantic?"

After hesitating a moment, the corner of his mouth crooked into a semi-grin. "Romantic."

Emma actually felt her heart thud to the ground at her feet. She should have seen this coming, but she was still taken aback by the idea of him dating someone. In all honesty, she was a little jealous of whoever the fortunate object of his affection was. "The Waterford Inn is really nice."

"You've been there?"

"No, but my parents celebrate their anniversary there every year. It's where he proposed."

"I love how your family keeps up their traditions," he said. "Not everyone does things like that."

"Thanks." She was dying to ask who he'd be taking to dinner, but it was absolutely none of her business. Besides, the very efficient Liberty Creek gossip chain would have that detail soon enough, and all she'd have to do was ask Gran. If she decided she even wanted to know.

"Emma?"

Startled out of her brooding, she forced her attention back to the handsome banker in front of her. "Yes?"

"You looked like you were a million miles away. Is everything okay?"

"Sure. What were you saying?"

"Asking, actually," he corrected her with one of the soft, genuine smiles she'd seen more of lately. "Would you like to have dinner with me there sometime this week?"

She stared up at him in amazement. "Me?"

"Of course you. Who else would I ask?"

"Anyone," she blurted, so stunned that she didn't even bother trying to keep her cool. "You could ask any woman within fifty miles, and she'd say yes in a heartbeat."

"That's very flattering, but I'm only interested in what you'd say. Unless you'd rather have some time to think it over," he added quickly.

His confidence seemed to waver a bit, and she realized it was because he was worried that she'd turn him down. He was so capable and strong, it was kind of cute to see him that way. "Yes."

"Yes, you want to think about it, or yes, you'll go?"

He looked so confused, she couldn't help laughing. "Yes, I'll go." Then something occurred to her, and she moved closer. "I know this is a big step for you. I'm honored that you'd ask me."

Gratitude flooded his chiseled features, and he gave her a gentle smile. "Thanks for saying that. Not everyone understands."

"I do," she assured him, resting an encouraging hand on his arm. "You should be proud of yourself for doing this. It can't be easy for you."

The smile warmed, and she saw that warmth reflected in the vivid blue of his eyes. "Actually, it's easier than I thought it would be."

"Why is that?"

"Because it's you."

He leaned in to brush a kiss over her cheek before strolling across the green to get back to work. She'd glimpsed tiny hints that there was more to Rick Marshall than met the eye, but she'd never been treated to a full-on display of his emotional side.

Now that she'd seen it, she didn't mind admitting that she liked it.

She liked it very much.

Chapter Eight

"Wow, Daddy," Caitlin approved from his open doorway. "You look really nice."

"Thanks, honey." Appraising his reflection in the mirror, he saw a guy who looked like he was walking headlong into something he wasn't all that sure about. Which made sense, because that was exactly how he felt. Pushing the negativity away, he turned to face his daughters and smiled. "It helps to have a woman's opinion."

"Emma will like it," Aubrey assured him.

"She already likes you," his older daughter pointed out with a conviction that he envied. "It doesn't matter what you wear."

"That works for kids, but grown-ups have to try a little harder."

Aubrey gave him a puzzled look. "Why?"

Rick started to reply, then realized he didn't have a good answer. Chuckling, he shrugged. "Because we do."

From the kitchen, Mrs. Fields called out for the girls, and after bookending him in a twin hug, they raced downstairs for the special meal she'd promised them. The scent of homemade macaroni and cheese and grilled hot dogs wafted up to him, and he was briefly tempted to invite Emma over for a more casual—and much less intimidating—dinner.

Feeling foolish, he shook off the uncharacteristic fit of nerves and pulled on the light suede jacket he hardly ever wore. The motion showed off a flash of gold on his left hand, and he reached down to spin Sarah's ring around his finger, thinking. Sam's terse suggestion echoed in his mind, but Rick was reluctant to remove it. He knew that once he did, he'd never put it back on again, and one of his precious connections to Sarah would be gone.

Debating with himself, he glanced at the photos on his dresser, lighting on one that always made him smile. It was of the four of them on a carousel at a park in Charleston. The girls were so small that he and Sarah held them on their ponies, and his mother had snapped the picture when they were all laughing. He remembered that day as one of the best in his life.

A year later Sarah was gone.

His cell phone rang, and he gladly took advantage of the distraction. When his mother's name showed up on the caller ID, he grinned at her innate sense of timing. "Hi, Mom. How're you today?"

"Oh, just fine," she drawled in a voice that had always reminded him of honey. "What are you up to?"

Rick was tempted to resort to the usual kid-centric update, then decided it wouldn't hurt to fill her in. "Actually, I'm getting ready for a date."

"With Emma, the art teacher?"

"That's the one."

"I'm so glad. You've been alone too long, and every time you talk about her, I can hear you smiling. As far as I'm concerned, the more time you spend with her, the better."

"What makes you say that?" he asked. "You haven't even met her."

"I don't have to. If she makes you happy, that's good enough for me."

The casual way she spoke about him being with a woman other than Sarah caught him by surprise. Then it occurred to him that she was right. No matter what his day had been like, Emma had a knack for making everything seem all right. Apparently, her upbeat attitude was contagious, because just thinking about her now was making him smile. "Thanks, Mom. The girls like her, too, which makes it easier."

"To take that step, you mean?"

"Yeah," he confirmed on a sigh. "It's a huge one for me."

"For anyone," she reassured him in a sage tone. "But once you make it, I think you'll be happy that you took the chance. Sarah would want you to have someone, for your sake and the girls'."

Those last few words stayed with him even after he finished their conversation and ended the call. Slipping the phone into his interior jacket pocket, he grasped the ring on his finger and closed his eyes for a moment, silently asking God to grant him some kind of sign. A light touch fluttered across his cheek, fading away almost as soon as it had appeared. The logical part of him dismissed the sensation as the breeze coming through his open window.

Another part, the one that Emma had redis-covered in him, knew that the touch had come from Sarah, kissing him goodbye so he could get on with the rest of his life. Before he could talk himself out of it again, he slid the wedding band from his finger and set it next to the frame that held the carousel photo.

After one last look at it, he turned and walked from the room. He wasn't completely certain of what lay before him, but at least his life wasn't stalled in the past anymore. Whatever happened between Emma and him, he'd always be grateful to her for giving him a reason to step out of the shadows and back into the light.

On the drive over to her house, he took a rare opportunity to admire the charming town that he and his daughters had found themselves in. The buildings were familiar to him now, but the change of seasons from winter to spring brought out different facets of it if you were looking closely.

The white gazebo in the town square had shed its white lights in favor of hanging baskets filled with flowers in vibrant shades of red, purple and pink accented with delicate white blossoms that cascaded over the sides in a waterfall of colors. Main Street shops stayed open later this time of year to accommodate the nicer evenings and seemingly endless flocks of tourists enjoying the beauty of the surrounding woods and untamed countryside.

Then there was the picturesque covered bridge the original Calhoun brothers had had the foresight to build generations ago. Practical by design, it also gave the town the lost-in-time feeling that Rick had first considered quaint but out of place. Now he found it as appealing as the rest of Liberty Creek, and he had to admit that the old-fashioned nature of the town and its residents had grown on him.

Pulling up to Emma's house, he admired the Craftsman style, built by hand years ago by someone who'd shown an admirable attention to detail. Being from Charleston, he had a healthy respect for history, but his own family heritage wasn't nearly as clear to him as Emma's was to her. That connection to the past was something his own girls didn't have, and as he went up the front walk, he resolved to do something about that sooner rather than later.

He lifted a hand to knock on the screen when Emma appeared on the other side, phone in hand. Holding up a finger for him to wait, she listened for a few seconds before speaking. "I understand, Dr. Finley. I'll be there Friday at three."

Her face was strained as she hung up, and

that old, helpless sensation clutched his heart in the kind of fear he'd experienced far too often with Sarah. Nighttime calls from a doctor usually signified bad news, but he didn't feel it was his place to ask her about it.

Apparently, she noticed his own somber expression because she gave him a soft smile as she opened the door for him. "Don't look so worried, Rick. I just have to go in for a bone marrow biopsy."

"To see if the leukemia is gone?" She nodded, and he let out the breath he hadn't realized he was holding until now. "What did your preliminary exam tell them?"

"I forgot you know all about this," she commented sadly. "It was encouraging, but Dr. Finley said the only way to know for certain is to do the more invasive test. They have to send the sample to a specialized lab in Boston, so it takes a few days to get the results. I like definitive answers, so I agreed to do it."

Rick knew only too well that "invasive" was an understatement for the painful procedure. Before he knew what was happening, he heard himself say, "You shouldn't try to drive after this one. I'll take you to your appointment."

"That's really not necessary. I'm sure my mom will do it."

For some reason he didn't quite understand, he wanted to be the one to be there for Emma. In spite of the fact that he was agonizingly familiar with what she'd be going through—or maybe because of it—he felt compelled to step in and do what he could to help her. "She lives in Waterford, so it would be a lot more driving for her to get you, take you to the hospital and bring you home. You and I can go there and back, which is just one trip. Unless you'd rather have her go with you instead," he added, just in case he'd overstepped some unseen line Emma had drawn for him to stand behind.

She studied him for a few moments as if she was trying to decide how to phrase what she wanted to say. "Not that long ago, you told me you couldn't go through that kind of thing again. I wondered about it when you asked me to dinner, but then I figured we'll have a good time and we have to eat somewhere. Taking me to the cancer center is something else again. Are you absolutely sure you want to take that on?"

"No," he answered truthfully, ignoring the dread he suddenly felt deep in the pit of his stomach. "But you've done so much for the girls and me, I want to repay you."

"I didn't mean to create an obligation for

you," she pointed out gently. "You don't owe me anything. Not even dinner."

Her mouth curved into an adorable grin, and it took everything he had not to kiss her then and there. It was so like Emma to shift from serious to teasing in just a few words, and it occurred to him that her buoyant attitude was the thing he enjoyed most about spending time with this remarkably resilient woman.

"Good to know," he replied, following her upbeat lead with a grin of his own. Holding out his arm, he asked, "Shall we?"

Laughing, she took his arm and strolled out to the car with him. "Do you know where we're going?"

"Sure. It's on my navigation system."

"Hmm…those things are notoriously unreliable out here. And most of the time, they take you straight to the highway and the most boring drive ever."

"And the quickest," he added, opening the passenger door for her.

"But you miss the pretty towns and winding country roads in between. Unless getting this evening over quickly is your plan."

"Not at all." After settling in beside her, he reached over to shut off the navigation screen. "You're in charge of getting us there and back."

"*I'm* in charge," she repeated with a smug look. "I like that. When you're the youngest in your family, it doesn't happen very often."

Chuckling, he started the engine and began following her instructions. He'd been to the neighboring small city of Waterford many times during the past few months, but never through it to the other side. They drove past several dairy farms and even got delayed behind a buggy being piloted by a woman in Victorian garb, complete with the biggest plumed hat Rick had ever seen.

"That's Moira Delaney," Emma explained, waving out the window as they slowly moved past a high-stepping horse the color of rich mahogany. "She competes all over the northeast in driving competitions. Her horses have won so many trophies and ribbons, she had to clear out a room in her house to display them all."

"We have a lot of buggies in Charleston, but they're mostly for the tourists," he commented as he turned in front of a lighted sign that read *Waterford Inn. Established 1872.* Pulling around the circular drive and into a free parking space, he asked, "Is everything around here from another century?"

"Pretty much. We're proud of our history,

so we take good care of it. If you don't, things start to disappear, and you can't get them back."

Intrigued by the comment, he shut off the engine and turned to face her. "That's a nice way to look at it."

"Is there another way?"

"Some people think it's better to keep moving forward, replacing old, broken-down things with new ones that work better. It's called progress."

"It's called shortsighted," Emma countered, a determined edge on her usually gentle voice. "You can't get anywhere worth being unless you know where you came from."

"'Those who don't learn from history are doomed to repeat it.'"

"Exactly. So you get what I'm saying."

He tried to smother a grin. "Yes, I do."

"Good answer."

"What would you say if I disagreed?"

Giving him a sugary smile, she batted her eyes in an obvious Southern belle impression. For his benefit, no doubt. "Take me home, kind sir."

Rick burst out laughing in a way that he seemed to be doing a lot more frequently since meeting her. Getting out of the car, he escorted her up the lighted brick walkway, pausing here and there while she pointed out some of the more intriguing features of the Federal-style building.

"It was a Calhoun cousin's private residence at first," she explained, "and then the man who built it died, leaving behind his wife, Felicity, and seven children. Back then this was a major crossroads through the area, so it was a busy place."

"Hard to imagine that now," he observed, looking around the peaceful clearing in the woods. The centuries-old pines shielded it from any traffic noise, providing a cocoon-like effect.

"Like we were saying earlier, things change. Anyway, the farm couldn't support them on its own, so she took advantage of the location and opened an inn for people traveling through here on their way to other places. Originally, she did all the cooking, and the family ate with their guests while the children did their schoolwork."

"Sounds nice."

"Doesn't it?" Tilting her head back, she took in a deep breath of the pine-scented air. "It's so pretty out here. The spot where Dad proposed to Mom is down by the pond. He kept getting interrupted by a very loud loon," she added with a laugh.

"Sounds like a great evening."

"It was. That's why they keep coming back."

Memories like that made up the patchwork of a lifetime, Rick mused as they continued up the walk and into the restaurant. Someday, the pain and grief would be behind him and he could get on with his life. Tonight felt like it might be the new beginning he'd been longing for.

And maybe, just maybe, he could finally stop stumbling over the past and move forward.

Emma couldn't eat another bite.

Setting down her fork on her delicate china plate, she sighed in contentment. "Don't tell Gran, but that's the best lemon meringue pie I've ever had."

"Mum's the word," Rick promised, winking at her in the sort of lighthearted gesture she rarely saw from him.

Now that she thought about it, though, he'd been doing more things like that lately. Maybe he was feeling more comfortable in Liberty Creek, now that he'd met more of the people who called it home. Whatever the reason, it was nice to see the lighter side of him more frequently. When their waitress brought over the check for their meal, he didn't even look at the amount before tucking his credit card into the leather folio that held their bill.

"Most people at least take a peek," she teased, taking a last sip of her tea.

"Whatever it is, it's well worth the investment."

Playing along, she asked, "Of time or money?"

"Both." He flashed her that elusive, playful grin she wouldn't mind seeing more of. After signing the credit slip, he tucked his wallet back into his inside jacket pocket and stood. "It's a nice night for a walk. Would you mind showing me around the grounds?"

"Not a bit," she replied, thrilled that he'd suggested prolonging their evening. When he pulled her chair out for her, she couldn't help admiring the old-fashioned gesture. Then again, she reminded herself that Rick Marshall had been raised to be a Southern gentleman. Those gallant manners probably came with the territory.

"So," she began as they went out the side door onto a brick patio, "what would you like to see first?"

"I keep smelling roses, so I'm assuming there's a garden around here somewhere."

"The original one," she confirmed, pointing to a sign with an arrow guiding visitors to its location. "It's away from the house, but it's worth the walk. There's even a maze done out of boxwoods. Felicity set it up to entertain her guests."

"Something to set this place apart from other inns and bring in the customers," Rick said in the tone of a businessman who appreciated the logic behind her approach. "Not many women back then thought like that. She was ahead of her time."

Emma wished her ancestor was here to take her bow. Since that wasn't possible, she accepted the praise and smiled. "Yes, she was. We Calhoun women can be very resourceful when we have to be."

"Your whole family is. Ellie's been successful doing what she loves. Sam's built a solid business as a contractor, and Brian's bringing the past right into this century. And you," he added, shaking his head. "You created an arts program from nothing, and kept it going out of sheer determination. None of that could've been easy, but you've all made great things happen for yourselves and the town."

Unaccustomed to praise for simply being herself, Emma wasn't sure how to respond. She wasn't as shy as she used to be, but sometimes she still found herself at a loss for what came next in a conversation. Fortunately, they were turning into the maze, and finding their way through the first jog gave her time to think. "You know all about my family and where I'm from. Tell me about Charleston."

"It's beautiful," he said simply, adding a nostalgic smile. "Lots of old houses, historic buildings and the harbor's full of every kind of boat you can imagine. Even you would never run out of things to paint."

"I've been to Boston a few times. Is it like that?"

"Sort of, but warmer and more laid-back. Plus, we have more crabs than lobsters."

Just thinking about the coastal town revived memories of the bustling wharf. From the unfamiliar sights to the briny scent of the daily catch, it was still one of her favorite trips. "I love fresh seafood, and watching the boats come in and out. Sailboats are so pretty silhouetted against the sunset."

"Spoken like a true artist," Rick said, reaching down to lightly take her hand in his. Raising their linked hands, he studied them for a moment, then chuckled. "Let me guess. Some of your students were painting sky scenes today."

Glancing down, she was mortified to see that she'd missed a good-sized swipe of pale blue on her wrist when she was cleaning up after her last class. She almost pulled her hand free, but something stopped her. She and Rick were friends, after all, so it wasn't a huge deal that he knew she wasn't perfect. Besides, her hand felt warm and protected in his larger one, and it felt nice to be connected to him in such a personal way.

So she did her best to laugh it off. "Yeah, it's an occupational hazard. Sometimes I don't get it all off. When I'm finishing up a fall landscape, my hands look like one of those camouflage jackets that hunters wear."

"I like a woman who really gets into her work." Beneath the teasing tone was a current of something Emma couldn't put her finger on. Then he stopped in the middle of the crushed stone pathway and turned to face her. Taking her other hand, he stared down at her with a look she'd never seen from him. When a corner of his mouth lifted in a half grin, she braced herself for yet another surprise from this man she thought she knew so well. "Especially when that woman is you."

Those compelling eyes held hers in a warm gaze that short-circuited her brain for a few seconds before she could get it going again. "I—well—what a sweet thing to say."

"You sound surprised."

"No, it's just—" He'd never looked at her this way, and she quite literally had no idea how to react. A few times she'd wondered how it would feel to be the object of this handsome man's affection, the woman he chose to share all his free time with. Now she knew, and it was at once exhilarating and terrifying.

"I can be sweet," he murmured.

Lifting her hands, he brushed his lips over the back of one and then the other in an unhurried motion that had the effect of turning her insides to mush. How he managed that, she couldn't say, but it was the most incredible thing she'd ever felt. A commanding kiss couldn't have touched her nearly as much as those gentle touches, and she couldn't keep back a sigh. "I know that, Rick. The first day in the park, when you helped me pack up my jewelry table and take it home, I knew."

Letting her hands drop, he slid his arms around her waist to bring her close. Male admiration glittered in his eyes, warming as he stared down at her. "How did you figure that out so fast? Most people never even think to look for that side of me, much less find it."

Bitterness edged his usually mellow voice, and it made her sad that he believed something so harsh about himself. But they both knew he was right, so there was no point in her trying to convince him otherwise. "It's just part of who I am, I guess."

"I guess it is," he murmured, leaning in to brush a kiss over her lips. He lingered for a heartbeat, then drew away slightly. It felt like a question, as if he was asking her permission to do it again.

Reaching up to his cheek, she drew him back in for another kiss. And there, in the rose-scented moonlight, in the middle of Felicity Calhoun's treasured maze, she lost her heart to Rick Marshall. It seemed appropriate somehow, because even while she cuddled into his strong arms, she knew only too well that she'd just stepped into a maze of her own.

A very personal, complex one, with plenty of blind corners that might very well end up winding around in circles with no solution in sight. But in this moment, they had tonight.

For someone who'd learned to live each day as it came, that was enough.

Rick hated hospitals.

Emma's oncologist had an office next to Waterford Memorial, and as they walked through the automatic doors, he took a moment to summon his considerable patience for what he expected to be a difficult visit. The lobby had a cathedral ceiling and skylights, which let even more sunshine into the surprisingly pleasant space. Painted a soothing gray, it was furnished with several styles of living-room-style pieces that gave the place a homey appearance. If it hadn't been for the wheelchairs in the entryway, he might have thought they were at a law firm.

Then a door opened, and a haggard woman shuffled through, supported by a younger woman who had an arm wrapped protectively around her. "I know that was tough, Mom," she said in a chipper tone that had a forced ring to it. "But you did great. How 'bout a milkshake?"

The older woman's sunken eyes lit up, and she managed a semblance of a smile. "Strawberry?"

As they made their way past him, Rick's

heart twisted with empathy for them. Cancer was a common foe these days. The worst thing was, you couldn't be sure that even your best efforts would be enough.

When he heard Emma's voice, it had a nudging tone that told him she'd been trying to get his attention. Turning to her, he said, "Sorry about that. What were you saying?"

"That I can have Mom bring me home so you don't have to stay. It might take a while, and I'm sure this is the absolute last place you want to be."

That she'd picked up on his mood was impressive. Ordinarily, he was able to mask his emotions around others, projecting a calm, self-assured demeanor that people appreciated in the man they'd put in charge of their money. Then again, he thought with honest admiration, Emma Calhoun was an extraordinary woman. It shouldn't surprise him that she'd see through his smooth act to what was going on underneath.

"I appreciate the offer, but I'll be okay." He waited while she checked in at the desk and then motioned for her to go ahead of him. Once they were both seated, he asked, "What gave me away?"

"The way you looked at that woman and her

daughter. Like you knew how they were feeling, and it made you sad to think of someone else going through that."

"It does make me sad," he admitted with a quiet sigh. Gazing over at her, he quietly added, "It's hard for anyone, even someone as brave as you."

That got him a peal of laughter. Several people glanced their way, and she blushed before continuing. "I'm not brave. I'm just doing what I have to do. It's either that or give up, and I'm not a quitter. I know that leukemia might get the better of me someday, but it won't be without a serious fight. Every year researchers come up with new treatments, and the chances of surviving improve. I put my life in God's hands a long time ago, and I trust His judgment about how long it will last. When you think about it, that's all any of us can do, cancer or no cancer."

Not long ago, hearing someone refer to the Almighty that way would have made him very uncomfortable, possibly even angry. Until now it had never occurred to him that God had taken Sarah when He did because it was her time to go. He still didn't understand why she had to die so young, but his recent exposure to religion had begun teaching him that things happened for a reason, whether he understood or not.

And in a flash of epiphany, the answer to that vexing question appeared in his mind as if someone had switched on a light. Swiveling to face Emma, he made a conscious effort to keep his voice low. Because he didn't know quite how to start, he just went for it. "I think I know why Sarah died when she did."

Sympathy flooded Emma's beautiful eyes, dulling some of their usual sparkle. "Why?"

"God knew how much she was going to suffer, and how hard it would be for our family to watch her keep getting weaker. He took her so she wouldn't have to fight so hard, only to lose in the end."

Straight from his heart, those words hung in the air between them for a few moments before drifting away. Reaching over, Emma clasped his hand in a show of support that very few people he'd ever known could manage.

"I think you're right about that," she agreed, adding a gentle smile for good measure. "Your family had suffered so much already, He didn't want you to continue on the way you were. Hard as it was to let her go, it was best for Sarah and you, and the girls, too. It gave you the chance to move forward and make a fresh start somewhere else."

With someone else, Rick added silently. It still felt odd to him, but that awkwardness was starting to fade, leaving him feeling grateful to this remarkable woman who'd reached out to him in friendship and was gradually becoming more to him than he could ever have imagined a few weeks ago.

Lifting her hand, he kissed the back of it before folding it into his. "Thanks for saying that. It must be weird to talk about a man's wife like that."

She gave him a quizzical look. "Not really. We've talked about her quite a bit."

"True, but things are different now." The puzzled look remained, and he worried that he might have misinterpreted their moonlit kiss the other night. "Aren't they?"

"Do you want them to be?"

Did he? Rick wondered, recognizing that this was his opportunity to disentangle himself from a woman who both enchanted and terrified him, depending on the situation. He treasured his time with Emma, but there were days when he questioned his sanity for breaking his own rule about pursuing a relationship with someone fighting the same disease that had broken his heart and devastated his young daughters by taking Sarah from them.

But in a flash of understanding, he realized that he didn't want an out. He wanted to be with Emma. He traced the curve of her cheek with his finger and smiled. "Yes, I do."

"That's good," she said, relief flooding those beautiful eyes. "Because I do, too. I just wasn't sure how you'd feel, now that we're sitting here, waiting for my test. Leukemia is sneaky, so I'll probably need to have more of them in the future," she added, clearly giving him one more chance to pull away from her.

Even though he knew her family would be around to support and encourage her, whatever the circumstances, Rick had no intention of taking her up on her very generous offer. Leaning in to kiss her cheek, he drew back to smile at her. "I know. I can take it."

Rewarding him with her most beautiful smile, she rested her head on his shoulder. "I'm glad."

They were still sitting that way a few minutes later when a woman leading a Golden retriever approached them. The dog wore a blue vest labeled Service and stopped when the woman did.

"Hello," she said in a quiet voice that made

him think of a librarian. "I'm Sandra, and this is Franny." She nodded at the dog, who sat politely in front of Emma with an expectant look on her face. It was as if she knew which of them was the patient, and Rick was amazed by the animal's perceptiveness.

"Hi, Sandra," Emma replied, adding a friendly smile. "I'm Emma, and this is Rick. It's nice to meet you." Franny offered her paw, and Emma laughed as she shook it. "And you, too, pretty girl."

"Franny's a comfort dog, and we volunteer here a couple times a week," the woman explained as she sat in the empty chair beside Emma. "Sometimes when people are nervous about their treatment, petting Franny helps distract them from what's coming."

"I'd think talking to you would help, too," Rick commented, surprised that she'd left that out.

"If they're up to it, sure. But some folks don't like to make conversation when they're upset. A dog doesn't expect anything other than to be petted, so often that's easier." Looking around the hushed waiting room, she smiled sadly before reconnecting with Emma. "My daughter lost her battle with cancer four years ago, and we spent a lot of time together here, talking or just sitting. Dreading the treatments, terrified of what the doctor would say."

"I know that feeling," Emma murmured, ruffling the dog's ear with a frown.

"It was awful, and that's when I got the idea of bringing Franny to help keep my daughter's mind off everything." Pausing, she chuckled. "At first, the staff thought I was nuts, but they decided that as long as our golden girl didn't cause any problems, it was okay. Other patients liked having her here, too. She's so sweet, it didn't take long to get her officially certified, and we joined a group of other animal owners who do the same thing. We go all over, trying to help where we can."

"Where else do you go?" Rick asked, fascinated by the concept of her giving up so much time to help strangers.

"Nursing homes occasionally, preschool reading groups, and yesterday we went to a school for special needs children. Once they got over their shyness, they just loved her. Franny was the runt of her litter, so she's on the small side for her breed. It actually works well, because kids aren't as afraid of her as they might be."

While the two women chatted, Rick noticed that she didn't ask any questions about Emma's

illness, or why she was here today. He suspected that it was because her mission was to
offer patients a distraction from their problems,
not drag them through their difficult personal
history. Normally, he was the kind of guy who
faced trouble head-on and figured out a way
to get through it.

But listening to them, watching Emma relax
and even laugh in spite of what was coming,
he began to see the value in a little escapism.
Most of the time she seemed to be accepting of
her situation, but Rick knew that for all her optimism, she still worried. He could see it in her
eyes sometimes, especially today. If Franny
could ease that relentless concern even briefly,
that was good enough for him.

During a pause in their conversation, he
fished a business card out of his pocket and
handed it to Sandra. "I'm the manager of Patriots Bank in Liberty Creek, and I'm always
on the lookout for local charities to support.
I think what you're doing is fantastic, and I'd
like to help you spread the word about what
you do. The more people who know about it,
the more donations you'll get."

"We're not a real charity," she protested, not
reaching for his card. "We're just people."

"People doing God's work," Emma reminded her with a smile. "Think how much more you could accomplish if you didn't have to fund everything yourselves. The training you did can't be cheap, and maybe if you could reimburse people for it, you'd attract more therapy teams."

Rick was stunned by the very pragmatic suggestion coming from the dreamy artist he'd been getting to know. Discovering that she had a practical side was a pleasant—and unexpected—surprise for him. It didn't escape him that her argument seemed to resonate with Sandra more than his had, and she finally took his card. "Thank you. Do you mind if I share your contact info with the group?"

"Please do. I'm happy to talk to anyone who does what you do. In my experience, people like that are few and far between."

"That's the truth," she agreed, shaking her head. "It's a shame, really. When you put aside your own problems and focus on helping someone else, it gives you a wonderful feeling inside. I've always thought that it's God rewarding you for following His wishes."

A nurse came out from the back and called Emma's name, so they said goodbye to Sandra and Franny and left the waiting room. As they followed the nurse down a hallway that led to the treatment area, Rick felt Emma tense up beside him and did his best to push down a sudden fit of uneasiness.

Maybe he wasn't ready for this, after all, he mused soberly. It had seemed a lot easier out in the lobby, when the impending test was a vague medical procedure that he didn't need to understand. Now that it was closing in on her, he got that old helpless sensation he knew all too well. Brave as she was, he knew that Emma was scared to learn the results of this latest biopsy.

And there was nothing he could do to take that fear away from her.

His derailing train of thought was interrupted by a small hand sliding into his as they walked. Soft and trusting, like a little girl seeking comfort for the ordeal that was rapidly approaching. His uncertainty evaporated, and he smiled down at her before resting an arm across her shoulders in what he hoped came across to her as a reassuring gesture.

Apparently, he hit the mark, because she rested her cheek against his chest, wrapping her arms around him in a sideways embrace that told him without words exactly how much his presence today meant to her.

Kissing the top of her head, he murmured, "You'll never have to do this alone, Emma."

Leaning her head back, she gave him a sweet, trusting look that sank deeply into his heart. "Promise?"

"I do. If they'd let me come in there with you, I would."

"That's a lovely thought," she said, the hint of a smile showing around her eyes. "But I'll pretty much be asleep. And I snore."

His laughter rang off the sterile white walls, and he hugged her close. The impulsive gesture was very unlike him, just one more way that Emma's approach to life had lightened his own outlook.

As he took his seat in yet another hospital waiting area, he watched her continue down the hall, chatting with the nurse while they went. Outside a doorway, Emma glanced back at him, and he forced himself to smile, adding a thumbs-up for good measure. The look she gave him was filled with gratitude, and she blew him a kiss before disappearing through the doors.

Suddenly alone, Rick swallowed down a knot of fear that was threatening to choke him. Rubbing his hands over his face to calm his nerves, he rested his head back against the wall and closed his eyes. The helplessness he'd experienced earlier returned in full force, but this time he knew what to do about it.

"Please, God," he whispered, "take care of her."

Chapter Nine

Tonight was the big night, and Emma couldn't believe how nervous she was.

She came to this school every day, she mused as she dragged her reluctant feet up the walkway that led to the front door. It was early June, and she'd started cleaning off the bulletin boards she'd designed for several of the hallways, returning the artwork to the students who'd been proudly displaying their work for everyone to appreciate. If things went well tonight, she'd be back for more of the same next year.

If not...

Rick had warned her that their grassroots campaign was a long shot, but during her long months of demanding chemo treatments, her faith had kept her going. She'd entrusted this problem to God, too, confident that He knew best. But she didn't mind admitting that if she lost her job, she was going to be incredibly sad.

When she walked into the meeting room, she noticed Rick standing at the front, talking earnestly with the school board members. Their somber expressions gave nothing away, although one of them was nodding as if she agreed with his argument. A last-minute pitch for saving their jobs, Emma assumed as she took an open seat near the back. She hoped that whatever he was saying was striking a chord with anyone who was still open to suggestions.

"Is this seat taken?"

Startled by the familiar sound of her father's baritone, she stood and embraced her parents. When she saw her brothers and their wives, and then Gran, a wave of gratitude flooded her heart. "What are you all doing here?"

"Where else would we be?" Mom demanded, stepping aside to let Chase into the row behind Emma.

"It's gonna be fine, honey," Gran assured her, patting Emma's cheek on her way past. "Things like this have a way of working out for the best. You'll see."

Emma noted that her very wise grandmother hadn't gone so far as to promise that at the end of the night, she and the others would still be employed. Only that the situation would resolve itself the way it was meant to. She could only hope that when she was older, she'd be able to view this kind of uncertainty with Gran's calm perspective.

As her family filled the row behind her, offering encouragement and hugs, she was reminded of how they'd always stood with her, through the good and the bad that had come into her life. Stalwart and determined, to her they personified the New England character that had built Liberty Creek and kept it going from one generation to the next. In all her life, she'd never been prouder to be a Calhoun.

Finally, Rick stopped speaking and went around the circle of administrators, shaking each of their hands before stepping away. His handsome features gave her no indication of how he thought the impromptu powwow had gone. But when he dropped into the chair beside her, she read his opinion in the tightness of his jaw. She had no idea what to say, so she waited for him to compose himself before turning to her.

"I don't know, Emma. I got the feeling they've already decided what they're going to do, but I ran every one of our points by them again, just in case some of them can still be swayed."

"I've known those people my entire life," she reminded him quietly. "Once they make up their minds, there's no changing them. They're conservative, thoughtful people who've always made sound decisions for the school, even when it's not easy to do. I'm sure they didn't take this one lightly."

"We gave them some solid options," he said in an optimistic tone that was clearly for her benefit.

"Yes, we did." Reaching over, she took his hand and smiled. "You did everything you could, Rick, and we're all very grateful to you for that. Without you, we wouldn't have stood a chance."

Out in the aisle, Dina and Christine paused to add their thanks before moving toward the front of the room to sit with their husbands and learn the fate of their jobs. Unaware of Rick's assessment, they looked a lot more positive than Emma felt.

Staring at them morosely, he let out a weary sigh. "They think I'm some kind of miracle worker. The problem is, I'm just a numbers guy."

"You're a lot more than that," she protested,

rubbing his shoulder in sympathy. "You use your brains and your business knowledge to help people solve problems, not just take care of their money. Being a banker is your job, not your whole existence. Anyone who's met your girls can see what a great father you are to them. That's a lot more important than anything you do when you're in your office."

"Yeah, it is." Slanting her a look, he mustered up a half-hearted grin. "Thanks for reminding me."

"Anytime."

Lending a hand to someone else is the best way to forget your own troubles, Gran always said, and Emma sat back in her chair, feeling good about lifting Rick's mood. When the large clock on the wall read seven, the school board took their seats and the president briskly called this year's most important meeting to order.

When everyone had settled, he got right to it. "I'm not going to waste anyone's time tonight. We all know why we're here." He quickly summarized the main topic of business for anyone who'd been living under a rock somewhere, and then he folded his hands in front of him in a humble gesture. "We had quite a bit of input from the town on this matter, and I want to assure you that we've taken every suggestion and criticism into consideration. One proposal from Rick Marshall—" he paused to nod in Rick's direction "—got us rethinking our approach to this issue, and I'm pleased to announce that as of about an hour ago, we've come to a tentative agreement with the Fairfield school district."

The crowd erupted like an excited beehive, and Emma's pulse sped up in response to the news. Nearby Fairfield was so small, it made Liberty Creek look like a boomtown. Years ago they'd been forced to end their arts and music programs to maximize their traditional academic offerings for their remaining students. She couldn't imagine what sort of compromise the two districts might have arranged, but she couldn't wait to hear the details.

She wasn't aware that she'd balled her hands into fists in her lap until Rick reached over and pried the fingers on her left hand open and took it in his own. Warm and strong, it closed over hers in a protective motion that made her feel that whatever was coming, it would be okay.

Once the initial excitement had died down a bit, the president held up his hands for quiet and went on, "There are some details we need to work out yet, but the gist of it is this. Fairfield and Liberty Creek will create three positions, one for an art teacher, one for music and another for a floating teacher's assistant. The people in these jobs will split their time equally between the two schools, with half of their salaries paid by Fairfield and the other half by Liberty Creek. We're still in the proposal stage at this point, but we—" he swept a hand toward the other members "—and our counterparts up the road are hopeful that this very practical idea will be approved and completely funded within the next few days. For now it will cover only the coming school year, until we can assess how well it will serve students in both schools. While we recognize that a more long-term solution is preferable, we feel that this is a good step forward for everyone involved."

Without any hesitation, Rick got to his feet and started clapping. Others immediately joined him, and before long, the entire assembly was applauding the school board, who totally deserved the adulation. Confronting a difficult issue head-on, they'd bravely stepped up and turned a fiscal defeat into a victory for not only the teachers whose jobs had been saved, but also the children in both schools.

Emma had seen and heard it for herself, but even as she cheered the decision, she couldn't quite believe it had actually happened. The two towns were about thirty minutes apart, so splitting her time between them would be a challenge, especially in the winter. But she didn't care.

She was going to stay in Liberty Creek and keep doing what she loved. In her opinion, life didn't get much better than that.

"What'd you tell them, Rick?" Brian demanded, a huge grin threatening to split his tanned face in two.

His question reminded Emma that the final solution hadn't been among the ideas their committee had come up with during their spirited debate in her living room. Realizing that Rick must have done something at the last minute, she waited for him to share his unexpected brainstorm.

"Well, I went back to my football days and called an audible." Giving Emma a rare hesitant look, he said, "It was a little off the beaten path, and I didn't want to get anyone's hopes up, so I kept it to myself. I hope you don't mind."

"Mind?" Laughing, she hugged him, then went up on tiptoe to kiss him soundly. They were in full view of about a hundred people, but she didn't care. Framing his handsome face in her hands, she shook her head. "You saved my job and two others, without taking anything away from anyone else. That's exactly what I told you I wanted, and somehow you made it happen. You're not only brilliant. You're a hero."

"Like Superman," Chase agreed brightly.

"I don't know about that," Rick hedged, giving Emma a sheepish grin. "Maybe Clark Kent."

"Whichever one you are, this calls for a big family party," Gran announced, extending her arms to include the rest of the clan. "Rick, go get your girls and bring them over to my house. Everyone else, come with me. We've got some celebrating to do!"

"We should have a cookout," Chase suggested to Sam, who chuckled.

"Sure, bud. We'll stop home and grab some hamburgers and hot dogs outta the freezer."

Chase whooped his approval, high-fiving Sam while Holly rolled her eyes at their boyish behavior. In the span of about a minute, a typical Calhoun picnic had been planned, and assignments were quickly taken up by whoever was best suited to handle them.

Once they'd all left, Rick turned to Emma with a baffled look. "Does your family do this kind of thing often?"

"Yes," she said, laughing. "Is it too much for a by-the-book financial genius like you?"

"Maybe," he replied, settling an arm over her shoulders to walk her out of the school. "But I'd imagine I could get used to it."

"That's good, because I really don't think you have much choice."

Rick was working his way through the bank's latest monthly reports when he heard a familiar chuckle in the doorway of his office.

"There's my favorite protégé," Charles Grumman commented in the booming Chicago-accented voice that was his trademark. "Hard at work making our customers happy and prosperous."

"Charles," Rick said, standing to shake his mentor's hand. "This is a great surprise. I had no idea the boss was coming by today."

"That was the plan. You know how I love popping in to catch my people slacking off."

More than once, Rick recalled that Charles had ventured into random branches dressed as a mechanic or a deliveryman, pretending to be a prospective customer. Sometimes he was pleased with the treatment he received, and sometimes not. But the ruse always gave him a genuine view of how things were running in the banks he owned. Rick admired the man as much for those visits as for his brilliant financial mind.

Motioning to a chair, he said, "Have a seat. Can I get you anything?"

"Answers," the robust man replied as he sat. "This branch is still fairly new, and I wasn't thrilled with the numbers they generated last year. That's why I sent you up here to get it whipped into shape. How are things running these days?"

That was a loaded question if ever he'd heard one, and Rick knew better than to go off-the-cuff when answering it. Besides, Charles had long ago taught him that demonstrating something to someone was much more effective than telling them about it. Spinning his monitor for his boss to see, he sat down and folded his hands on the leather blotter in a casual, confident pose. "See for yourself."

Pulling a pair of wire-rimmed reading glasses from his jacket pocket, Charles put them on and stared at the screen, touching tabs here and there to access different sets of figures. After a couple minutes of that, he removed his glasses and leaned back in his chair to give Rick a keen-eyed once-over. Rick knew better than to speak at this point, since the intense scrutiny was aimed at seeing if the owner's target would start to squirm. Another tactic Rick had learned from the master himself.

Finally, the older man casually set his left leg across his right knee, resting over it a hand that sported a gleaming diamond-studded wedding band and a watch that had cost more than Rick's car. "I'm impressed. I didn't doubt that you'd find a way to boost this place, but I wouldn't have expected even you to get it going so fast. What's your secret?"

"Getting to know the people here has made all the difference," Rick answered truthfully. "It's a great community, full of hardworking, honest people who want to build a better life for their families. Their financial needs aren't huge, but they're important, and folks tend to honor their obligations."

"That kind of accountability is pretty rare these days. What do you think makes these customers different?"

"Pride. Some of these families have been here for generations, and they're planning to stay for generations to come."

Charles gave him a long look, then nodded. "So keeping this branch instead of selling it off was a good idea, after all. I was beginning to wonder."

"Not to brag, but I told you that last fall."

"Yes, you did." His boss chortled, then sobered in a way that alerted Rick their conversation was about to shift onto a different track. "Well, you honored our deal and righted this sinking ship for me. Without your expert touch, this place would be closing at the end of the quarter. I'm grateful for your help."

Rick recognized that tone, and his pulse picked up speed before he settled it back down with a quiet breath. "I'm grateful for the opportunity you gave me to prove myself."

"I know that." After a pause he went on, "Aside from your professional accomplishments, your loyalty and willingness to live in the middle of nowhere all this time mean a lot to me personally. So I have a new assignment for you. How does Charleston sound?"

Rick's heart leaped at the thought of returning there, being near his family, raising his girls in the warm, sunny home he'd always longed to go back to. But there was a hitch. "We don't have a branch in Charleston."

"Patriots Bank has a presence in all of the

original thirteen colonies except for South Carolina. I want to put you in charge of fixing that."

"You mean I'd be the branch manager?" When Charles nodded, Rick swallowed to be sure his voice wouldn't crack from the excitement coursing through his body. He had a reputation for being cool and steady no matter the circumstances, and he didn't want to ruin that by being impulsive. "I'm honored that you'd consider me for such an important position."

The bank owner smiled at him as if he knew exactly what Rick was thinking. Fortunately, he didn't chide him for hiding his true feelings about the offer. "You've earned it, and more. Just how much more will depend on how well things go down there."

The tantalizing promise of a future promotion made it even tougher for Rick not to jump in and take the job, but he managed to keep calm. At least on the outside. "I understand. It's better to make an assessment of the local environment and then see where we should go from there. When would this assignment start?"

"I know you've got a daughter in school here. When is she done?"

"Kindergarten graduation is in two weeks,"

Rick replied, grinning at the amused look on his boss's face.

"My grandson had his last year. Be on your guard—they do their best to make the parents cry."

Rick laughed. "Thanks for the warning."

"Anyway, if you're ready for work by July first, that'll be fine. That gives you time to get settled and make sure the girls are comfortable before you start. Once a proper site is located and purchased, we'll be putting up our own stand-alone building using local contractors and suppliers. That will ensure buy-in from the community and hopefully encourage them to get in line as our new customers. I want you on site every day, overseeing their progress to make sure they stay on track." Standing, he extended his hand again. "I've contracted with a human resources firm to expedite the hiring, but you'll have the final say on your staff. I have every confidence that you'll get it right."

He didn't wait for a decision, or for Rick to ask for time to make one. As Charles strode from the office on his way to go torment some other poor, unsuspecting manager, it was obvious that he fully expected the offer to be accepted, and gladly. For Rick, the path ahead wasn't quite so clear.

Closing the door, he returned to his chair and rocked back into his heavy-thinking pose. The colorful landscape that brightened the mundane room caught his eye, and he swiveled to gaze at it, hoping to find some inspiration in the tranquil scene.

His career had taken him up and down the East Coast, so he'd moved often enough that he had the process down pat. The thought of doing it again didn't bother him, particularly because he knew that, this time, Charleston was waiting for him at the other end. While that appealed to him, he and his girls had made some wonderful friends here, and had become attached to the residents of this quirky little town in the middle of the New Hampshire woods.

Especially Emma.

He could no longer deny his growing fondness for the soft-spoken teacher who'd brought so much into his life. Not to mention, she'd come to mean a lot to his daughters, who adored her in a way he'd never anticipated. He tried to envision what it would be like never seeing her, sharing a walk around the square or meeting her at Ellie's bakery for lunch. It was no surprise for him to discover that he couldn't do it.

Instead, his imagination inserted her into some of his favorite old haunts, marveling at the treasures hanging in one of the art galleries to be found throughout the downtown district, or touring The Charleston Museum with her and his daughters. It was easy to think of her drinking in the rich history of his home the way she'd so generously shared hers with him. And that was when it hit him.

Maybe she'd like Charleston. The vote for her job had gone better than he'd anticipated, but there was no guarantee that the school boards would continue their experiment beyond the coming year. That would leave Emma in the same trouble she'd just come through, and next time there might not be a remedy for it. During his career, he'd learned that most fiscal problems never really went away. They just morphed into something slightly different down the road.

One of his longtime friends was the headmaster of a private high school near the large suburb of Mount Pleasant. Was it possible that they were looking for an art teacher?

Deciding that there was no time like the present, Rick pulled up the contact list on his phone and found the right number. When his old buddy picked up on the first ring, Rick summoned a casual tone and returned the greeting. "How're things down there?"

"Hot and sticky," Peter drawled with a chuckle. "How 'bout up there in your neck o' the woods? Run into any bears yet?"

"Hardly." Rick heard his own Low-Country accent creeping in and remembered Emma's comment about how nice it sounded. Grinning at the memory, he charged ahead. "I know someone who might be relocating soon, and I'm wondering if Franklin or another school in the area might be needing a teacher."

"That depends. What kind of teacher?"

Duh, Rick thought with a mental forehead slap. Apparently, thoughts of Emma had short-circuited his usual sharpness. "Art."

There was an awkward pause, and Rick worried that he'd lost the connection. Then he heard a knowing laugh on the other end. "How pretty is she?"

Busted, he thought with a grimace. Then, because it was Peter, he laughed, too. "Very. Her name is Emma Calhoun, and she's great with kids of all ages, from kindergarten right up through high school. She has her master's in art education, and she's incredibly talented."

"Anything I might've seen?"

"I doubt it, since she's from New Hampshire." The canvas hanging on his wall caught his eye again, and he said, "Hang on a second." Snapping a picture, he sent the photo to his friend. "Did you get it?"

"Wow," Peter breathed in obvious appreciation. "If it looks like this as a digital image, it must be amazing in person."

"It is. Whattya think?"

"I think I need to meet this woman. We don't have a spot currently, but if she's as great as you claim, I'm sure we can make one."

Private schools, Rick thought in relief. The big ones like Franklin had deep pockets and more leeway on spending decisions than public districts. If Emma got a job there, it would be as secure as anything could be these days. "I was hoping you'd say that."

"When you get down here, let's get the families together at our place for a good, old-fashioned barbecue."

"Sounds great. Thanks a lot, Peter."

"Sure and done," he replied in one of the high school phrases they'd invented. Rick echoed it and ended the call with a smile.

The past few years had been full of challenges for him and his daughters, and the going had been pretty rocky for them at times.

Maybe now, things were finally changing for the better.

And if Emma was part of the picture, then everything would be perfect.

Excited by the prospect of grabbing that elusive brass ring, he glanced at his watch to find that it was almost noon. He called up Emma's number and waited for her to answer. When she did, he opened with, "What are you doing for lunch today?"

"Nothing. Why?"

"Can you meet me at the bakery in about ten minutes? I've got something to discuss with you, and it can't wait."

"Ooo…sounds mysterious," she teased. He could imagine those incredible blue eyes twinkling in fun, and it occurred to him that he was officially a goner. "Can you at least give me a hint?"

"Nope. See you in a few."

Rick closed his laptop and his office door, feeling as if he was on top of the world. All of his hard work, the sacrifices he'd made, were about to pay off in the best way possible. Even agreeing to Charles's oddball request to move to the middle of nowhere and take over a struggling New England branch now looked like a shrewd career move rather than an insane leap into the abyss. Loyalty meant everything to his boss, and while Rick would have taken the Liberty Creek assignment without the promise of a better post later, it was gratifying to know that personal integrity still had value for some people.

It was a nice day, so he decided to walk the few blocks to meet Emma. As he approached Ellie's Bakery and Bike Rentals, he recalled the bleak afternoon when he first drove into this little town several months ago. It was a bitter January day, and after crossing the landmark covered bridge, he'd been baffled to find this oddly named business in the center of town. Inside he'd discovered a woman who seemed to consider herself everyone's grandmother and had charmed his tired daughters with milk and cookies fresh from the oven.

The lady herself was behind the counter when he strolled in, and she came around to greet him as if she hadn't seen him in ages. After a warm hug, she asked, "How's my favorite businessman today?"

"Hungry, and something smells fantastic. What is it?"

"My latest culinary invention," she replied, adding a wink and a smile. "I think you'll like it. Why don't you try it and let me know what you think?"

"Sounds good," Emma said from the doorway. "Make it two."

Beaming at her granddaughter, Ellie folded her into an emotional embrace, holding her tight before letting her go. "Anything for you, my sweet pea."

Rick had a feeling something was going on, but he knew it wasn't his place to ask about it. As the talented cook hurried into the kitchen to get their order, he motioned Emma to a table for two near the window. Before they sat, she turned to him and said, "I'm actually glad you got in touch with me earlier. Dr. Finley called with the results of my last test this morning. As of today, my leukemia is in full remission."

Rick let out an uncharacteristic *whoop*, sweeping her off her feet for a joyful hug. Setting her down, he grasped her arms as he fought off the urge to kiss her. They were in a public place, after all, and he knew it was important to behave with some sort of decorum. "Emma, that's fantastic! Judging by the way she greeted you, I'm assuming Ellie knows about it."

"I called everyone in the family as soon as I heard, but I wanted to wait and tell you in person. Since you went to the appointment with me, I thought it was the least I could do."

Once they were seated across from each other, she rested her arms on the table and leaned forward eagerly. "Now that you've heard my news, what's up with you? You look like you're about to burst."

That was exactly how he felt, but for once he didn't bother wondering how she knew that. Despite the calm demeanor that he'd always prided himself on, Emma had a knack for reading his moods, both good and bad. Instead of trying to explain it, he decided to accept her uncanny perceptiveness and forge ahead. "I had a visit from my boss this morning."

While he filled her in, she followed along with nods and an occasional comment about how wonderful it all sounded. If she believed the professional aspect of the offer was good, he thought with anticipation, wait until she heard the rest.

"But that's not even the best part."

"You and the girls moving home to Charleston? What could be better for you than that?"

Reaching over, he took her delicate hands in his and steadied his voice before answering. "I want you to come with us."

Her eyes widened in astonishment, and she

blinked at him a couple of times as if he'd completely lost his mind. "You…what?"

When it occurred to him that they'd only recently begun dating, he realized how his crazy suggestion must sound to her. Feeling foolish for jumping the gun that way, he backed up a step. "Not to live with us, but on your own. I know you'd love it down there, and I'll help you find a nice place near Charleston."

She let out a noncommittal sound, and he forged ahead. "A good friend of mine is the headmaster of a private school down there." He went on to relate their discussion, and how excited Peter was to meet her in person.

"I can't imagine why. He has no idea who I am."

"I told him all about you, and he was very impressed. Besides that, you're young and dedicated, and you're not only a great teacher, you're a really talented artist."

Now her eyes narrowed suspiciously. "How does he know that?"

"I sent him some pics of your work. The landscape that hangs in my office, other pieces you've shown me at your house that I took pictures of. He'd really like to meet you and talk about you taking a job at Franklin."

"But I have a job," she pointed out, clearly

bewildered by the whole thing. "The one you worked so hard to help me save last week. Remember?"

"That's a one-year contract," he argued sensibly. "This time next year, you could be facing the exact same problem."

"Or I might not. Whatever happens, I'll cross that bridge when I get to it."

"I appreciate that attitude, but Franklin is an amazing institution that prepares kids for Ivy League colleges. Here, they're just…" A warning flashed in her eyes, and he slammed his runaway mouth shut before he blundered into saying something that would make this normally sweet-tempered woman angry.

"Just *what*, Rick? Two small schools in the middle of Nowhere, New Hampshire? Not important enough to be taken seriously?" Her voice rose, and she pulled her hands away from his before standing to her full height. Which wasn't that tall, but the fury sparking in her eyes as she glared down at him would have made anyone think twice about taking her on.

"I am a teacher," she reminded him in a lethally cool tone that made his skin crawl. "And nurturing students means everything to me, no matter how many of them are in my classroom. The kids in Liberty Creek and Fairfield are every bit as important as the ones in some private school for families who can afford to give their children virtually anything they want. Thank your friend for his interest in me, but I won't be going to Charleston. Or anywhere else, for that matter."

With that, she spun on the balls of her pink ballet-style shoes and marched from the bakery without a single glance back at him. Rick sensed that someone was standing behind him and braced himself as he swiveled to find Ellie holding two platters of today's special.

Feeling like a moron, he sighed. "I guess you heard that."

He half expected her to set down the plates and leave the way her granddaughter had, but to his surprise she put them on the table and sat down across from him. "I'm not usually one to eavesdrop, but this place isn't that big, so it was hard not to. I don't mean to pry, but I have one question for you."

"Sure."

"What on earth were you thinking?"

She sounded more confused than angry, which Rick took as a good sign. "I was thinking that this is the big promotion I've been working toward for the past five years, and it's finally here. Then I was thinking about how much I hate winter."

Ellie smiled, and then pinned him with a knowing look. "And?"

She already knew what he wasn't saying, Rick realized, and while he wasn't keen on sharing his feelings with anyone just now, he recognized that it was pointless to pretend that they didn't exist. "And I don't want to leave Emma behind. She means a lot to me, and to the girls."

"She means a lot to her family, too," Ellie pointed out calmly. "Did you consider that, in asking her to move so far away, you'd be putting her in the position of choosing between us and you? Not to mention leaving the job that she loves so much. I know you didn't intend to upset her, but quite honestly, I don't blame her for storming off like that."

Frowning, she patted his hand and headed back to the kitchen. Rick stared at the delicious-looking lunch she'd left him but didn't think he could get it past the knot in his throat without choking. Ellie was right, he grudgingly admitted as he left money for their lunches under the sugar shaker and stood. He'd been so thrilled about making a professional change, he'd assumed that Emma would be as eager for one of her own.

He trudged out the front door, pausing on the sidewalk to take in the normally peaceful village around him. The sound of a loud conversation up the street got his attention, and he looked in the direction of the forge to find a loaded-down pickup parked out front. Obviously worked up over something, Brian was jawing with a tall man who stood with his arm around a very pregnant red-haired woman.

Rick's curiosity got the better of him, and he headed up the sidewalk to find out what was going on.

"Jordan, I always thought you were the smartest of us cousins, but now I'm not so sure. Why didn't you tell anyone you got married?" Brian demanded, sounding equal parts astonished and angry.

So this was Jordan Calhoun, Rick thought, the wayward cousin Brian had been waiting for most of the year. The plan was for him to join the staff of Liberty Creek Forge as an artisan and turn his expertise into one-of-a-kind iron pieces for their customers. When it dawned on Rick that he was intruding on a sensitive family moment, he stopped in his tracks and did his best to ease back the way he'd come. But his presence hadn't gone un-noticed, and he found himself caught in the crosshairs of Brian's sharp gaze.

"Don't run off, Rick," he called out, wav-ing him over. When Rick joined them, he went on, "I want you to meet my cousin Jordan. He might be a moron, but you gotta admit, he has excellent taste in women."

"Don't make me pound you," the tall artist threatened, although the mischievous twin-kling in his hazel eyes gave away the fact that he was joking. Thrusting out a scarred hand, he said, "Jordan Calhoun. And this is my wife, Ainsley."

"My pleasure, both of you," Rick answered, shaking their hands. "Welcome to Liberty Creek."

"See?" Jordan said to his cousin in an ac-cusing tone. "That's how you greet someone who's just gotten into town."

"Whatever." Turning to Ainsley, he gave her a patented Calhoun grin. "You were telling me how you two met."

"At the Faire," she replied in a lilting Irish accent that was at once unique to this place but somehow seemed right at home. "I make costumes and sell them to the entertainers and fairgoers. Jordan had damaged his antique leather vest during a demonstration and asked if I could repair it for him. And the rest, as they say, is history."

She rested a maternal hand over her plump waistline and beamed up at her husband, who returned the look without hesitation. When Brian's wife, Lindsay, appeared in the open doorway of the forge with their daughter in her arms, Ainsley lit up in delight.

"Is this Taylor?" Lindsay nodded, and she went on in a gushing tone, "She's growing up so fast! In the pictures Jordan showed me only a couple of months ago, she was just a baby."

"It's our fault," Lindsay joked, laughing. "We keep on feeding her."

"She's the most beautiful thing I've ever seen," Ainsley complimented them, taking the hand that Taylor held out to her for a gentle squeeze. "It's amazing to me how perfect such a tiny person can be."

"It sure is," Brian agreed, giving his cousin a less stern look. "So now that the shock has worn off, you have to tell me what you're doing here. I wasn't expecting you until the fall."

"It's my fault," the expectant mother explained with a frown. "We planned to work the rest of the Faire season and then come here to surprise everyone. I still think we should have done that," she added, slanting a disapproving look at her husband.

"The baby's due in September, and I didn't want Ainsley working those long hours outside in the heat that far into her pregnancy," Jordan said in an even tone that clearly told them that he'd had to put his foot down for the good of his spirited wife. "So we both finished up a few outstanding contracts we had, and here we are."

"I still can't believe it," Brian commented, shaking his head. "After all those years of wandering around the country like a gypsy, you're finally gonna settle down."

"Can't think of a better place to do that," Jordan said, looking around him with a satisfied expression. "This place is like a living piece of history, and I'm looking forward to raising our family here."

Any other time, Rick would have felt odd being included in such a personal conversation. But as the three of them discussed children and the Calhouns' legacy blacksmith shop, it occurred to him that they weren't including him just to be polite. It was because Brian viewed him as a close friend and felt comfortable talking in front of him this way. Once the conversation shifted to catching up on Calhoun news, though, Rick felt that it was time to go.

"Jordan, it was great meeting you and Ainsley. I hope we'll see each other again soon."

"At Gran's for Sunday dinner, probably," the artist said, shaking his hand.

Assuming that he was still invited, Rick thought as he turned and headed back to the bank. Emma had been furious with him at lunch, and he wasn't sure where he stood with her at this point. As he walked, several people stopped to chat with him, thank him for his help in getting them a loan or commend him for his work at the school.

The sensation of belonging in this charming hamlet hit him, and not for the first time. When had it started? he wondered, searching his memory for the answer. When he found it, he wasn't surprised to discover that Emma was involved. That day in the town square, when he stopped to see his daughter's favorite teacher and purchased some jewelry for Mother's Day. It didn't seem like that long ago, he mused, but in some ways, he was a different person then.

Emma had brought out a part of him that he'd put away years ago, reluctant to risk losing himself in someone else who might leave him too soon. He liked the changes that he saw in himself, but for longer than he could recall, it had been his dream to be in charge of his own bank. Being the boss, choosing his staff and in this case, even the decor that would surround his customers on a daily basis.

The trouble was, his daughters had blossomed here in Liberty Creek, and while they were familiar with Charleston, these days their visits to his hometown were short and full of grandparent time. He knew that if he was going to move them, he needed to do it now before Caitlin became too attached to her classmates. And Aubrey. His timid little girl, who took so long to open up to anyone, had flourished here with Emma and the friends she'd made in Sunday school. So the choice was a simple one, but also the hardest one he'd ever had to make.

Stay in Liberty Creek, happy in his personal life but already at the top of his professional ladder? Or move back to Charleston and fulfill a goal he'd set for himself when he entered college at eighteen?

Emma had made her position painfully clear, and while he wished that she'd reconsider, he respected her choice. Envied her, in fact, because she hadn't had to mull it over for even a second.

Unfortunately, his situation was more complicated, which made his decision more difficult. And this time, he didn't think one of his pro-con lists was going to help.

Chapter Ten

Two long, difficult weeks later it was time for kindergarten graduation. Since her blowup with Rick, Emma hadn't spent any time with Caitlin outside school, and she hadn't seen Aubrey at all.

And Rick. When she saw him, it was in passing, usually as he drove by in his car on his way to somewhere. Whether he noticed her or not, she couldn't say, but he didn't acknowledge her, so she'd been left to assume that their tense conversation at the bakery would be their last. After getting so attached to the Marshalls, being so distant from them was a difficult adjustment for her to make.

Once they were gone, it would be easier, she reasoned as she sprinkled more sugar over a tray of Gran's famous cinnamon twists. At least that was what she kept telling herself. Fortunately, she wasn't the only Calhoun woman on the food committee, and her family's lively conversation was a welcome distraction from the darkness of her mood lately.

"How're you doing, sweetheart?" Mom asked, giving her shoulders a sympathetic squeeze.

"Fine."

"I know that kind of *fine*," her mother teased, laughing. "It doesn't work any better on me now than when you were little and had a bad day at school."

Emma shrugged and focused on her task as if it was the most important thing she had to do.

"I know it's hard, but he'll be gone soon," Lindsay said in an obvious attempt to make her feel better.

She wasn't one to brood, but her lunchtime encounter with Rick—someone she thought she knew well—had left her so rattled, she still hadn't gotten over it. When she recalled how it had gone, she got mad enough to chew iron and spit out nails. The old-fashioned saying had been one of Granddad's favorites, and while it didn't often apply to her, in this case she thought it summed things up perfectly.

"It was like he never even met me," she fumed, stabbing a poor, defenseless pig in a blanket with a toothpick to hold it closed. "What on earth would make him think that I'd leave my family for a job teaching a bunch of rich strangers' children a thousand miles away?"

"Challenge?" Holly suggested while she slathered icing on a batch of sugar cookies. "Money? I hate to say it, Em, but South Carolina is beautiful, and Charleston is downright breathtaking. All that history, and the grand old buildings. I actually think you'd like it there." Emma glared across the table at her sister-in-law, who shrugged. "Just being honest, honey. I mean, here you're already on top of the mountain. At a bigger school with better funding, you'd have opportunities that you could only dream about here."

"Money isn't everything," Gran pointed out as she pulled a tray of fresh biscuits from the cafeteria's oven. "I think our girl should do what she thinks will make her happy. Whatever that is," she added, tapping Emma's head with an oven mitt.

"May I say something?"

Ainsley had been silent up till now, artfully decorating cookies made in the shape of graduation caps while the rest of them had been complaining about the general cluelessness of the male species. When she spoke, Mom laughed. "Of course you can. You don't even have to agree with any of us if that's what you're worried about."

"Well, my grandmother—God rest her— used to say that if you're doing something strictly for money, it might make you happy for a while, but not for long. She was a maid for a wealthy family in Dublin her entire adult life, and although she made good money, she detested going to that job every single day. So I'm thinking she knew what she was talking about."

"That's the truth," Lindsay put in, scowling at some unpleasant memory or another. "I can't tell you how many idiots I made look good while I was a temp at those law firms. I saved the bacon of at least a dozen Harvard graduates, and they treated me like the dirt under their shoes."

"Now you're a full-fledged partner in the family business," Holly reminded her brightly. "You've come a long way."

"And you run your own design firm," Mom commented proudly. "Not to mention you two keep my stubborn sons in line and make them happy at the same time. I don't know how you manage it."

That was what she wanted, Emma thought with a mental sigh. She had a fulfilling career and was surrounded by an amazing family that supported her no matter what was going on. But there was something missing from her life, and as she'd grown closer to the Marshalls, she'd gotten a glimpse of what else she might be able to have. The trick was for her to find the courage to reach out and grab it.

"Mom?" Her mother glanced up and prompted her to go on. "What do you think I should do?"

"Well, that depends. How interested are you in trying something new in a different place?"

"I'm not sure. It's kind of intimidating to think about leaving home. What if I'm terrible and the kids hate me?"

"What if you're fabulous and they love you?" Holly asked in her usual pragmatic way. "And for the record, I think it's great that Rick went to the trouble of setting up that interview for you. Men don't do things like that unless they're serious about you."

Emma had to admit, the way Holly phrased it made it sound really sweet. Since their romantic dinner and first kiss, he'd definitely been more attentive to her, and she'd begun to wonder if they'd make a good couple. Sadly, his proposal at lunch the other day had set her off, and she hadn't reacted well to it. Now that he'd backed away from her so completely, she wasn't at all certain that she could make things right again.

While she was brooding, Mom said, "It's not like he asked you to move in with them. He suggested that you might like to try making a new life for yourself in Charleston, where he and the girls will happen to be living. As for the different school, you'll never know how it will work out unless you try."

"But I don't want to leave Liberty Creek," Emma protested, stubbornly holding her ground in a circular argument that she suspected she couldn't possibly win. Because debating with yourself usually turned out to be a pointless exercise in frustration.

"Then stay," Lindsay advised. "If you decide to take the leap later on, there are plenty of fancy private schools out there who'd jump at the chance to hire you."

Suddenly tired of the discussion, Emma thanked her and picked up a tray to carry into the gym where the reception was being held after the brief ceremony.

It felt very strange to be discussing another job when she was getting ready to celebrate kindergarten graduation day, one of her favorite events of the school year. She always got a little choked up, but usually she comforted herself with the knowledge that she'd be seeing the kids again next year as first-graders, so the day was a bittersweet one.

This time Caitlin Marshall was leaving for good, and Emma wouldn't be able to see her grow up and turn into the amazing young lady God had obviously designed her to be. As if that wasn't bad enough, Aubrey, who had more creative talent in her little finger than a lot of folks ever showed, would never be part of her class. Emma wouldn't be surprised if the shy, sensitive child eventually grew into a remarkable talent who would go on to wow people with her art.

And then there was Rick. Just when they seemed to be getting closer, he'd shown her the side of himself that had made people mistrust him when he first came to town. More banker than art lover, that very businesslike man wasn't someone she was interested in spending any more time with than absolutely necessary. The art lover, however, appealed to her tremendously.

Her internal debate came to a screeching halt when she turned to find the object of her confusion standing a scant couple of feet away. Her current frame of mind must have been showing on her face, because he held up his hands in front of him in the surrendering motion she recognized from when her brothers were attempting to appease their wives.

"I didn't mean to startle you, Emma. One of the other teachers told me I'd find you in here."

Her thoughts were so topsy-turvy that she had no clue how to respond. Then, from out of nowhere, she heard herself blurt out, "Where's Aubrey?"

Apparently, that wasn't the reaction he'd expected, because he frowned. "In the auditorium with Mrs. Fields. Why?"

"No reason. I was hoping to see her."

"You can," he replied with one of those dashing smiles of his. "We'd be happy to have you sit with us during the ceremony."

"I'll be on stage with the rest of the staff."

"Oh, right."

Totally out of place with his personality, his downcast expression made her regret her curt tone, and her conscience nudged her to try to smooth things over. "I'll be in here afterward. We can all get together then, if you want."

"Is that what *you* want?"

Was it? she asked herself. Ever since their disastrous conversation at the bakery, she'd wrestled with the choice he'd presented her, trying desperately to come up with an answer she felt good about. One minute she thought she'd never leave her hometown. The next she thought a new challenge was just what she needed. And that if she didn't take this shot at this point in her life, she wouldn't get another chance at it.

But for now she simply addressed the question he'd asked. "Sure. That's fine."

Even she heard the tepid nature of her voice, and judging by Rick's tight smile, he heard it, too. "Then I guess we'll see you later."

He turned and began striding away, his long legs making short work of the distance to the hallway. Emma opened her mouth to call him back, then closed it before she had a chance to make a complete fool of herself. Rick's dream was to run his own bank, and he'd worked hard to put himself in a position to make it come true. As a lifelong dreamer herself, she'd never do anything to ruin someone else's.

But as he left the gym, she wished that there was a way for them both to have what they wanted. Unfortunately, for them to be together, someone would have to give up something incredibly important to them. It was obvious to her that Rick had made his decision, and she was the last person who'd try to talk him out of it.

Right now she had a celebration to enjoy. Or at least pretend to enjoy, she amended with a sigh before plastering a smile on her face and heading back to the kitchen for more treats. This was a big day for the kids, and she wasn't going to spoil it by fixating on her grown-up problems.

There would be plenty of time for that later when she was alone.

Rick understood that this wasn't a full-on graduation ceremony, but he didn't mind admitting that it was more emotional for him than he'd anticipated. He didn't know if it was the other parents around him trading nostalgic comments about their kids' first year of school or his awkward encounter with Emma, but he was definitely not his usual even-keeled self. Fortunately, Caitlin stopped to say hello on her way into the auditorium and pulled him out of the strange mood he was in.

"I like your hat," Aubrey said, hands folded in front of her politely while she admired the paper graduation hat Caitlin had decorated in Emma's class. Complete with a tassel made of silver tinsel, it gave him a glimpse into the future when his girl would be graduating from high school. And then college. And then…

Rick stopped himself before he had her married and a mother of three. Out of consideration for the very short attention span of the graduates, the lighthearted ceremony lasted about fifteen minutes. When it was over, the principal thanked everyone for coming and encouraged them to stop in for some treats before heading out. Then the kindergarteners filed out, waving to their families on their way into the gym.

Caitlin met them there, and when she took off her hat and placed it on her younger sister's head, Rick's heart felt like it would burst with pride.

"That was a nice thing to do," he approved, hugging her around the shoulders proudly.

"In a couple more years, you'll have one of your own," she told Aubrey.

Beaming up at her, his youngest said, "And I'll let you wear it."

"Thanks, Froggy."

"Sure. When you're nice to people, they're

nice back, right, Emma?" she asked as the pretty teacher came over to join them.

"That's how it's been for me, anyway."

Delighted to see her as usual, the girls wrapped her in a double hug, and she reached her arms around to bring them in closer. It didn't take a genius to notice that the embrace went on longer than usual. Rick's chest constricted a little at the sweet sight, knowing that in all likelihood it was the last moment like that they'd share.

"We're going to see Gramma and Grampa on Saturday," Caitlin told Emma, clearly excited by the prospect. "We get to go on a big plane and everything."

"That sounds like fun. And much faster than walking all the way to South Carolina."

"Walking," Aubrey echoed, laughing. "You're so funny."

She really was, Rick acknowledged, remembering times when Emma's sense of humor had not only surprised him but also lifted his spirits at the end of a tough day. That was how she'd endured her cancer and its grueling treatments, he knew. That and the faith she'd taught him to appreciate so much that he couldn't imagine living without it again.

"So your parents must be thrilled to have

you coming home," she commented, finally including him in the discussion.

"Yeah, they are. I'm leaving the girls with them while I do some site work and find us a house. The movers will take care of this place and shipping my car, so that's everything."

"I'd imagine being so organized helps make things easier."

It felt like he was having this discussion with a mildly interested stranger instead of a woman he'd grown so fond of over the past couple of months. She'd done so much for him and his girls, he thought as the two of them raced away for some of Ellie's kid-friendly finger food. He couldn't leave without finding out what he'd done to sour everything just when the future seemed to be coming together for them.

Stepping closer, he kept his voice low to avoid having anyone eavesdrop. "Emma, I know this isn't the right time, but I have to ask. What did I do wrong?"

"Nothing." At first, she seemed prepared to leave it at that, then continued in a sad murmur. "You're a great guy, but I think you and I want different things out of life. It's better to find that out now rather than later, don't you think?"

"Is this about the Franklin job? Because you don't have to interview for it if you don't want to. I promise, I wasn't trying to pressure you into doing anything you're not ready for."

"I know." Patting his arm, she gave him a melancholy smile. "We need more punch, so I'm going to go mix up some more. Have a good trip."

As she walked away from him, Rick couldn't help feeling that there was something he could do to smooth things over between them.

But for the life of him, he couldn't imagine what it might be.

It was a beautiful day at the end of June, and during her morning walk, it occurred to Emma that her leisurely tours of the town just weren't the same anymore.

Emma sighed as she rounded the corner that led to her house, reminding herself that letting Rick go had been the best option for both of them. Since making that fateful choice in the middle of the school gym, she'd alternated between gloomy and regretful, finally landing on resigned. Because she trusted in God's wisdom, but she was still human enough to wish that things might have gone differently for them. She was also human enough to question why He'd brought them together only to allow them to break apart later on.

Approaching her front yard, she was surprised to see someone sitting on the steps, scrolling through screens on a cell phone. When her visitor lifted his head, she let out a shriek that got her neighbor's beagle barking.

"Rick!" Without thinking, she broke into a run and threw herself into his arms as he stood. Recovering a bit, she pulled back and tried to remember that she was supposedly an adult. "I thought you were in South Carolina. What are you doing here?"

"I figured out what I did wrong."

"What?"

Wrapping his arms around her, he reeled her in for a kiss that literally took her breath away. When he broke the kiss, he drew back but kept her neatly circled in his arms. "I love you, Emma, and I don't want a life without you in it. Here, Charleston, Jupiter, where we are doesn't matter to me, as long as we're together."

Her heart soared at those words, and she felt as if her face would split open with the smile she couldn't contain. "I love you, too, and I'm so glad you came back. I was starting to think

I made a huge mistake in giving up on us the way I did."

"Well, now," he drawled, flashing her the roguish grin she adored. "That's good to hear, because the girls and I have a question for you."

Pausing, he nodded to something behind her, and Emma turned to find Caitlin and Aubrey emerging from behind the trunk of the massive tree in her front yard. They came forward, stopping on either side of their father in a sweet group that brought tears to her eyes.

And then Rick went down on one knee, holding up the most beautiful ring she'd ever seen. "We love you, Emma Calhoun. Will you marry us?"

Emotion clogged her throat, and she couldn't speak, so she simply nodded. She ignored the tears streaming down her cheeks as he slid the ring onto her finger and raised her hand to his lips for a kiss. After a moment she finally found her voice. Gazing at him, this wonderful man who'd faced down his own demons to love her, she cradled his cheek in her hand and smiled.

"I love you, too. All of you," she added, reaching out to gather his daughters into the circle.

"We're going to make an awesome family," Caitlin announced confidently.

"You know what?" Emma said, laughing. "I think you're right."

Epilogue

Rick wore a tie to work every day, but this morning for some reason, his fingers wouldn't work properly. He stood in front of the full-length cheval mirror in one of Ellie's pretty guest rooms, sighing as he undid the knot—again—and started over.

A low chuckle sounded in the doorway, and he angled a look over his shoulder to find three Calhouns dressed in their Sunday best staring in at him.

"Are you new at this or what?" Brian teased, sauntering into the room with his usual confident stride.

"I never wear those things," Jordan chimed in as he sprawled out across the foot of the bed in the kind of casual pose that seemed to be wired into his laid-back personality. "They're a pain."

"Holly did mine for me," Sam said, motioning for Rick to spin around to face him. "You can copy hers if you want."

"Very funny," Rick shot back, turning to look in the mirror. Then again, it wasn't the worst idea he'd heard, even if its purpose was to make fun of him. "Is she up here, by any chance?"

"Downstairs wrangling the kids into place," his tall brother-in-law-to-be informed him. "Seeing as Emma's kinda busy."

"It's been like that all month," Rick complained, although he couldn't help smiling. "She's always wanted an outdoor fall wedding, and when she's not putting together favors for the guests, she's been glued to the weather forecasts. I know Ellie has room for everyone indoors, but I'm glad we got such a nice day."

"I'm glad we can finally stop monkeying with the backyard," Jordan groaned. "I've done enough mowing, planting, weeding and raking to last me a long time."

"Hey, you wanted to come home," Brian chided, tossing a throw pillow at his head.

"Yeah, I did. Now that we've got baby Henry with us, I'm surer than ever that it was the right decision."

Rick remembered that new-father feeling, equal parts pride and joy, knowing that all of a sudden he was responsible for the well-being of a tiny, helpless person. "Where you raise your kids makes a huge difference in their lives. My girls love it here, and I'm sure Henry and his future siblings will, too."

"It's a great place to grow up, that's for sure," Jordan agreed, rolling off the bed to get to his feet. "I'm gonna go check on Ainsley, so I'll see you guys downstairs."

After he'd gone, Rick got the impression that there had been some kind of secret signal among the cousins that had prompted the lanky artisan to leave. Bracing himself for whatever might be coming, he faced Emma's protective older brothers squarely. "Something you want to say?"

"He's good," Brian commented, motioning for Sam to go ahead.

In his usual direct way, the former Ranger got right to the point. "In the past, we've given you a hard time on occasion."

"*Every* occasion," Rick corrected him good-naturedly.

A slow grin worked its way across Sam's features, and he went on, "But it's easy to see how much Emma means to you, and we've never seen her happier. So we just wanted to officially welcome you to the family."

He held out a large hand scarred from count-less scrapes and knocks, and Rick accepted the gesture without hesitation. Working with Brian on his business had netted them a friendly ca-maraderie, but Sam had always been more of an enigma for him. While Steve and Melinda had accepted him easily, it was Sam he'd al-ways wondered about. Now that he knew where they stood, he felt his jangled nerves settling nicely into place.

"All right, then," he announced, rubbing his hands together eagerly. "Let's go have the kind of wedding Emma's always wanted."

Because he couldn't possibly choose be-tween them, the two brothers were his best men. Pastor Welch was already in the yard that Jordan had put so much effort into, stand-ing under an intricate arbor Jordan had made and Ainsley had strung with garlands of fall flowers. The charming setting was flanked by two rows of chairs from the church with a wide aisle in between. A white runner ran up the opening, and he smiled when he saw

Chase escorting his famous grandmother to a seat right up front.

Daphne paused on the nearly full bride's side, then glanced back at Rick with a thoughtful expression. Granting him an almost playful smile, she walked over to the groom's side and sat down next to his parents. Their eyes widened in surprise when they recognized the retired film star, and nearly popped out of their heads when she introduced herself to them as if they had no clue who she was.

As he walked past her on his way up to the lectern, he leaned in and whispered, "Thank you."

She waved off his thanks but winked at him as if she understood how it felt to be outnumbered and in need of a little reassurance.

Once everyone was in their seats, Mrs. Welch began playing a classical piece on her portable piano, and the guests turned, looking expectantly toward the back of the outdoor chapel. Caitlin came first, carrying her bouquet just so and looking incredibly grown up in the fluffy pink dress that seemed to float on the breeze. Taylor squealed in delight, and Lindsay hushed her, handing her a stuffed giraffe to keep her occupied.

Ellie was stationed at the back, shepherding people in from the rear porch door as they emerged, and he wondered if she'd have to nudge Aubrey into place. To his relief, his not-so-shy youngest stepped forward on cue, smiling at each guest as she scattered red rose petals on her way to the front, where matron of honor Holly gave her a quick hug.

Then the piano sounded those famous wedding chords, and everyone stood as Emma appeared with her parents on either side of her. She paused for a moment, looking up into the flawless autumn sky with a grateful smile. She mouthed a thank You, and Rick silently added his sentiments to hers.

God had answered so many of his prayers recently, sometimes Rick wondered what he'd done to deserve that kind of grace. But as his future wife made her way up the aisle to stand beside him, the only thoughts he had were of her and the life they were about to have.

Steve and Melinda each hugged her before stepping back and sitting with the rest of their clan. He noticed them exchanging looks with his parents, who still seemed to be a little bewildered by the fact that Daphne Mills was sitting beside them at their son's wedding.

"Friends and family," the pastor began, holding out his arms to include everyone, "I want to welcome you to this beautiful day the Lord has granted us for this very joyous occasion. The joining of two remarkable people, Emma Calhoun and Richard Marshall."

Rick heard a giggle and out of the corner of his eye saw Aubrey cover her mouth with her hand while Caitlin elbowed her in the side. They didn't often hear him referred to by his given name, and apparently it had struck her as funny. Not surprisingly, Emma smiled over at her, letting her know that her humorous outburst was okay with the bride.

This was the woman he'd chosen to love for the rest of his life and help him raise his daughters, Rick thought fondly. If he'd kept searching for years, he couldn't have possibly found anyone more perfect.

After a brief homily about the solemn promise they were about to make to each other, the pastor took Emma's wedding ring from Sam. Handing it to Rick, he asked, "Richard Allan Marshall, do you take this woman, Emma Jean Calhoun, as your lawfully wedded wife?"

"I do," he replied, sliding the band into place with her diamond.

Handing Rick's ring to her, he asked, "Emma Jean Calhoun, do you take this man, Richard Allan Marshall, to be your wedded husband?"

"I do."

Once she gave Rick his ring, the pastor closed his Bible and announced, "I now pronounce you man and wife. You may kiss the bride."

Rick leaned in to do just that, but was interrupted by his suddenly impetuous daughters breaking free of Holly to circle Emma and him in a jubilant double hug.

"We're a family!" Caitlin exclaimed, tossing her bouquet in the air for whoever wanted it.

"Daddy?"

Hearing Aubrey's voice, he bent down to pick her up, assuming she was feeling overwhelmed by all the excitement they'd had today. "Yes, sweetness?"

"I'm hungry."

"That's okay, because Grandma Ellie made us a fantastic lunch."

"Oh." Clearly disappointed, she fixed him with one of those looks he could never seem to resist. "But it's a special day. Can we have cake first?"

Emma burst out laughing, and Rick threw his head back and laughed in a way that he was looking forward to doing a lot more of. Gazing over at his new wife, he cocked his head and grinned. "What do you think, Mrs. Marshall?"

"I think it's time for cake."

If their guests found the arrangement odd, no one said anything as they fell into line behind the new family and followed them to the linen-draped table that held the beautiful four-tier wedding cake Ellie had made for them.

"Is this how you pictured our marriage beginning?" he murmured to Emma while they both grasped the antique cake server and posed for pictures.

"Truthfully?" When he nodded, she stood on tiptoe to kiss him. "I never pictured it any other way."

* * * * *

Dear Reader,

This is the final Liberty Creek book, and I couldn't think of a better way to end the Calhoun family's heartwarming story.

When Emma Calhoun appeared in the first book of the series, I liked her right away. Her quiet strength and resilience in the face of such a serious illness amazed everyone around her, and her unwavering faith was truly inspiring. Being creative and playful in a situation like hers isn't easy, but those traits made her a great teacher and just the kind of person Rick needed in his life. For him—as for so many—regaining his emotional balance after the tragic loss of his wife felt almost impossible. Emma and his sweet, funny daughters showed him the way, and fortunately he was open-minded enough to follow them.

Maintaining a positive attitude during tough times in our lives can help us to accept what's happened in the past and move ahead. While today might look bleak, tomorrow things will be better. No matter how slowly we seem to be going, moving forward is the important thing, because going backward simply isn't an option. While I didn't intend for this concept to be the theme of this series, it definitely became the unifying aspect of all three stories.

Our history makes us who we are, and the future is something for us to reach toward. The present is where we make our true impact, as we go through each day doing the best we can with the circumstances we find ourselves in. Liberty Creek—and the people who live there—embody this idea perfectly. I hope you've enjoyed this charming place, with its frozen-in-time appearance and its warm, friendly people. I know I did.

If you'd like to stop in and see what I've been up to, you'll find me online at www.miaross.com, Facebook, Twitter and Goodreads. While you're there, send me a message in your favorite format. I'd love to hear from you!

Mia Ross

Get 4 FREE REWARDS!

We'll send you 2 FREE Books plus 2 FREE Mystery Gifts.

Love Inspired® Suspense books feature Christian characters facing challenges to their faith... and lives.

FREE Value Over $20

YES! Please send me 2 FREE Love Inspired® Suspense novels and my 2 FREE mystery gifts (gifts are worth about $10 retail). After receiving them, if I don't wish to receive any more books, I can return the shipping statement marked "cancel." If I don't cancel, I will receive 4 brand-new novels every month and be billed just $5.24 each for the regular-print edition or $5.74 each for the larger-print edition in the U.S., or $5.74 each for the regular-print edition or $6.24 each for the larger-print edition in Canada. That's a savings of at least 13% off the cover price. It's quite a bargain! Shipping and handling is just 50¢ per book in the U.S. and 75¢ per book in Canada*. I understand that accepting the 2 free books and gifts places me under no obligation to buy anything. I can always return a shipment and cancel at any time. The free books and gifts are mine to keep no matter what I decide.

Choose one: ☐ **Love Inspired® Suspense Regular-Print** (153/353 IDN GMY5)   ☐ **Love Inspired® Suspense Larger-Print** (107/307 IDN GMY5)

Name (please print)

Address   Apt. #

City   State/Province   Zip/Postal Code

Mail to the **Reader Service:**
IN U.S.A.: P.O. Box 1341, Buffalo, NY 14240-8531
IN CANADA: P.O. Box 603, Fort Erie, Ontario L2A 5X3

Want to try two free books from another series? Call 1-800-873-8635 or visit www.ReaderService.com.

*Terms and prices subject to change without notice. Prices do not include applicable taxes. Sales tax applicable in N.Y. Canadian residents will be charged applicable taxes. Offer not valid in Quebec. This offer is limited to one order per household. Books received may not be as shown. Not valid for current subscribers to Love Inspired Suspense books. All orders subject to approval. Credit or debit balances in a customer's account(s) may be offset by any other outstanding balance owed by or to the customer. Please allow 4 to 6 weeks for delivery. Offer available while quantities last.

Your Privacy—The Reader Service is committed to protecting your privacy. Our Privacy Policy is available online at www.ReaderService.com or upon request from the Reader Service. We make a portion of our mailing list available to reputable third parties that offer products we believe may interest you. If you prefer that we not exchange your name with third parties, or if you wish to clarify or modify your communication preferences, please visit us at www.ReaderService.com/consumerschoice or write to us at Reader Service Preference Service, P.O. Box 9062, Buffalo, NY 14240-9062. Include your complete name and address.

LIS18

Get 4 FREE REWARDS!

We'll send you 2 FREE Books <u>plus</u> 2 FREE Mystery Gifts.

Harlequin® Heartwarming™ Larger-Print books feature traditional values of home, family, community and most of all—love.

FREE
Value Over
$20

HOME on the RANCH

YES! Please send me the **Home on the Ranch Collection** in Larger Print. This collection begins with 3 FREE books and 2 FREE gifts in the first shipment. Along with my 3 free books, I'll also get the next 4 books from the Home on the Ranch Collection, in LARGER PRINT, which I may either return and owe nothing, or keep for the low price of $5.24 U.S./ $5.89 CDN each plus $2.99 for shipping and handling per shipment*. If I decide to continue, about once a month for 8 months I will get 6 or 7 more books, but will only need to pay for 4. That means 2 or 3 books in every shipment will be FREE! If I decide to keep the entire collection, I'll have paid for only 32 books because 19 books are FREE! I understand that accepting the 3 free books and gifts places me under no obligation to buy anything. I can always return a shipment and cancel at any time. My free books and gifts are mine to keep no matter what I decide.

268 HCN 3760 468 HCN 3760

Name _____ (PLEASE PRINT)

Address _____ Apt. #

City _____ State/Prov. _____ Zip/Postal Code

Signature (if under 18, a parent or guardian must sign)

Mail to the **Reader Service**:

IN U.S.A.: P.O. Box 1867, Buffalo, NY. 14240-1867
IN CANADA: P.O. Box 609, Fort Erie, Ontario L2A 5X3

* Terms and prices subject to change without notice. Prices do not include applicable taxes. Sales tax applicable in NY. Canadian residents will be charged applicable taxes. This offer is limited to one order per household. All orders subject to approval. Credit or debit balances in a customer's account(s) may be offset by any other outstanding balance owed by or to the customer. Please allow 3 to 4 weeks for delivery. Offer available while quantities last. Offer not available to Quebec residents.

HRCBPA18